REHOBOTH REIMAGINED

REHOBOTH REIMAGINED

Presented by
Rehoboth Beach Writers Guild

The stories and poems within are entirely the imagination of the talented members of the Rehoboth Beach Writers Guild. Names, characters, businesses, places, events and incidents are either the products of the author's imagination or used in a fictitious manner. Any resemblance to actual persons, living or dead, or actual events, is purely coincidental.

The Rehoboth Beach Historical Society and Museum has granted the Rehoboth Beach Writers Guild permission to use the photos in this book; reproduction of photos is strictly prohibited.

CONTENTS

ACKNOWLEDGEMENTS

This anthology would not be possible without the Rehoboth Beach Historical Society and Museum and in particular, Director, Nancy Alexander. Many thanks for opening the Museum's photo archives to the Rehoboth Beach Writers Guild.

Generous donations of time, leadership and literary mastery were made by the *Rehoboth Reimagined* Editorial Board: in particular, the Rehoboth Beach Writers Guild Founder, Executive Director and voice of inspiration, Maribeth Fischer; as well as Ethan Joella; Sarah Barnett; Linda Blumner; Bonnie Walker; and Denise Clemons. This book would not be possible without their collaboration. Thank you.

Express thanks to designer Crystal Heidel for volunteering her graphics talents to create an intriguing cover for this book.

Special thanks to Steve Robison for taking on the physical publishing aspects of this project and to Mary Harris for her eagle eye.

Most importantly, continuing gratitude to the Guild members who spent time and creative energy to dream, write and submit works for this book. All of the members of the Rehoboth Beach Writers Guild bring their unique perspectives and talents to each of our endeavors, so we can only expect even greater works in the future.

Cynthia Hall
Editor

INTRODUCTION

Credit where credit is due: The idea for this book was inspired by Alexander McCall Smith's 2015 publication *Chance Developments: Stories* (Pantheon Books) within which he created fictional stories based upon unattributed vintage photos supplied by a curator.

What better place than Rehoboth Beach, Delaware to revisit turn of the 20th Century history in the form of fictional stories. And how lucky are we to have the wonderful Rehoboth Beach Historical Society and Museum collection to inspire the members of the Rehoboth Beach Writers Guild.

The pictures chosen for this anthology are unattributed, with no clear provenance, and used with explicit permission of the Rehoboth Beach Historical Society and Museum. The writers understand that the people photographed are someone's relatives—even though the pictures are unattributed—and have therefore taken great care to be respectful of the persons depicted. Be assured, all stories within are complete fiction and bear no relation to the real people photographed.

Please enjoy these imaginative stories and poetry and the flavor of seaside Rehoboth Beach, Delaware at the turn of the 20th century.

Cynthia Hall
Editor

1. TRAIN

Photo Courtesy of Rehoboth Beach Historical Society and Museum

All the best
Kathleen Marden

The Time of His Life

by Kathleen L. Martens

Great Grandpa Henry King was none of those things—not great, not Grandpa, and definitely not a king...except for once.

Mother took in the old, bent gentleman after the tragedy. The automobile accident that stole the lives of his only son and daughter-in-law had left him without care. We found him on that same windy summer day, unresponsive as he'd always been, rocking on our neighbor's porch in his handmade wicker chair waiting for their return.

The Kings had only moved next door to us a short time before this poor soul lost his only living relatives. We didn't know a tad about the old man, not his age, not his history, nor his pedigree, no clues that weren't in the outdated clothes and the leathered wrinkles of his face and hands. We were neighborly, not nosey.

"God planted the desire in my heart," Mother had said. "I can't call myself a Christian or a Methodist if I don't take him in." As the daughter of a founder of The Rehoboth Beach Camp Meeting Association of the Methodist Episcopal Church, Mother's faith was deep, and she lived her words. There was no argument from Father; there never was. And that was that. She made the arrangements, and Great Grandpa Henry King moved to rock in his chair on our front porch, as though he had always been a part of our family.

Mother fed him; Father kept him clean, groomed his bushy handlebar mustache, and parted his hair in the middle, the comb following a stubborn, well-worn groove from another time. My brother and I competed to see who could make him talk or move, or smile. His stiff collar and bow tie style were decades behind the times. No matter how hot the summer days became, he wore his oversized suit with dignity, the excess of his shirt escaping through the missing button on his vest. We imagined he must've been a big man in his time, his body withering to frail from sitting.

It was 1928 when he moved in. I'm sure of that. June 17th, the very day Amelia Earhart crossed the Atlantic on my twelfth birthday. Just a few years after they paved that beautiful road from Georgetown and built the new drawbridge over the canal into town that made the automobile ride into Rehoboth a pleasure.

That same year, we took Great Grandpa Henry King on his one and only excursion to the main street to see the last passenger train leave our Rehoboth Station. They were closing down the line. He preferred his special perch on our porch, but the mention of the train's fate was enough to spur him to join us.

The way that sight got Great Grandpa King's attention, got my attention. He stared down the empty tracks waving long after the locomotive's black cloud of steam was gone, and we had to drag him in the other direction home. It was the last time he'd go into town. That image, the slump of his shoulders, and the gray cast that came down on his eyes as the train pulled out of the station stayed with me for years.

It was a memory I took out and brushed off every time I rode a train.

I don't remember him ever speaking, but once. But each day, no matter if the sun rose up or the clouds dropped rain, he hobbled down the three blocks to the beach, took in three deep breaths of the salty air, and trudged along the shore until he found a perfect, intact seashell. I never knew what it meant to him, but he buffed that shell on his shirt like shining an apple, and placed it in a wooden fruit crate he kept in his room beside the old iron bed.

Once Mother or Father planted him in his chair on the porch to enjoy the day, Great Grandpa Henry King sat there quietly, his gray hair lifting with the ocean breezes in two pieces, like wings of the complaining gulls that hovered above. He had a kindly silence about him, with a touch of sadness.

"Shall I read to you?" I asked, sitting on our porch rocker beside him. I couldn't stand him sitting all alone, so I did the only thing I knew to do. Sometimes I read my school lessons, a few pages from our story books, or a parable from the family Bible. From the first time I read to him and every day after, when I finished the last word of a book, he'd push himself up with his shaking arms on the rocker, amble into the house through the creaking screen door, and return with one of his treasured shells. He held it up, kissed it goodbye, patted my head, and handed it to me smiling. In turn, I sneaked back into his room, and feeling the burn on my face for intruding on his privacy, I replaced it deep in his collection so he wouldn't notice. It was just that way he looked at those shells that made me know they were precious friends, or held a memory for him. Or maybe it was simply all he had to give. And thus our circle of giving went on.

He sat quietly, except for three times a day at exactly the same times when he waved his hand at some invisible crowd, and smiled. His eyes saw something I couldn't see; they lit up, showed a kind of joy, then faded right back to gray. I kept track. He was like a statue or a frozen mime, a coo-coo clock's bird until he came alive at 8:22, 11:22, and 5:52.

I worried about him sitting in the blazing sun, staring off across the ocean, dull-eyed. At the end of each day, after he took in the last bastion of angled sun, after he smelled Mother's apple pie, or shrimp and grits through the screen door, but just before he came in for supper, he saluted, nodded his head, looked up at a certain spot in the distance, and smiled.

———————

I felt sad leaving him when I went off to get my teacher training in Philadelphia. The memory of his moist eyes as I left him inhabited me for days. Unpacking my things at the house where I would live for the year of schooling, I'd found a perfect conch shell nestled in my satchel—smooth and pink inside and stark white on the outside. Nothing was as steadfast as that sweet old man. He was like an anchor in my life, my silent, great grandfather clock.

I wrote postcards every day; mother read them to him. With my mind on my studies, time passed through a full cycle of seasons quickly, and it was time to return. On my way home on the train, the memory resurrected—his eyes and his face years before at the sight of the last locomotive shrinking off into the foggy distance where the tracks seemed to merge into a mere pencil line pointing into the horizon.

When I returned to town to take a teaching position at our local school, I became obsessed with the very thing that we all came to take for granted since my childhood—Great Grandpa Henry King's mysterious rhythm, the wave and smile that still went on and on like clockwork after ten years.

I began my research though I had no idea just what I was searching for. A schedule? For what? Not any repetition I knew, not any local train schedule, not a factory whistle pattern. I became determined. Our retired postmaster, nearing ninety, was my first stop. I smoothed my floral dress to cover my knees, and sat on his porch rocker. "I'm looking for clues to the meaning of the pattern of Great Grandfather's, well…habitual happiness." The entire town had witnessed it over the years. "Would the times, 8:22, 11:22, and 5:52 mean anything to you?"

"Not our schedule," the postmaster said. "Trains were on the half-hour every third hour precisely, in season. Less frequent in the winter."

I explained my passion to know more, but he only said, "It's just what the man does. Why not try Widow Smyth? She's been around since day one."

She knew nothing. Great Grandpa had been a newcomer, after all. And so it went with every elderly soul in Rehoboth, no answers, but quite a bit of tea. The answer wasn't in our town.

When the school year ended, I took the train to Philadelphia where I stayed with my cousin for ten days. I pored over newspapers, and consulted with historians, genealogists; I had to solve the mystery of the man who rocked on our front porch, the curious timing of his reliable wave and smile, and his sadness at the last train departing from Rehoboth that remained fresh in my mind and still made my chest ache.

Tracing the King family was impossible, such a large Irish clan they had in the U.S. There were lists of James Kings, and Henry Kings. None fit.

On the day before I planned to leave, a librarian suggested another source—a Mr. Jonathan White at the Pennsylvania Railroad antiquities office. He knew trains like family members. Intrigued with my quest, he stayed late into the night searching for clues to Great Grandpa's life, and he found the thread I sought. A schedule of the stops on the train from New York to Philadelphia to Washington, D.C., 8:22, 11:22, and 5:52. I had to turn my back to hide my tears.

The next morning, I stopped by on my way to the train to thank him. There, with papers scattered over his desk, and the scent of bitter coffee in the air, I found a disheveled Mr. White with a wide grin on his face. He handed me his most important discovery. The sun angled through the oversized soot-streaked windows of the office onto the yellowed newspaper article, my pot of gold. My hands shook so hard the print blurred.

March 10, 1888

Engineer James Henry King ended his thirty-four years of service to the Pennsy today. "I've never wrecked a train, and I've never injured a passenger," he was quoted as saying on his last but prestigious run to Washington, D.C. on the Congressional Limited Express. King carried a very special passenger that day, President Grover Cleveland. When asked by a young reporter, "How does it feel to have a President as a passenger?" Mr. King responded with a laugh, "Maybe we should ask how the President feels about having a King for an Engineer?"

I laughed as I read Great Grandpa King's answer. To finally attribute a sense of humor to the enigmatic gentleman on our front porch was a delight, and I hugged the article to my chest. He'd retired just one day before the Great Blizzard of 1888, forty years before he arrived on my porch, keeping his record of no wrecks, no injuries. I would never know his exact age, not knowing when he started his railroad tenure, but by my figuring he could have been as much as a century old.

After making a purchase in the railroad antiquities gift shop, I secured the photo taken of President Cleveland with Great Grandpa King in front of his locomotive from the newspaper published on that day in 1888, and a copy of the schedule from New York City to Washington. I traveled home, my stomach fluttering all the way, knowing he'd time and again beheld the very scenery passing before my eyes from his front train window.

Great Grandpa Henry King was rocking according to schedule when I arrived. He stood and extended his arms holding a box containing ten perfect shells, one for each day

I was away in Philadelphia. How long his quiet days must have seemed to him; how fast the time had flown for me.

I strapped the souvenir Pennsylvania Railroad Commemorative wristwatch on his arm, kissed his cheek, and showed him the photo and the schedule at exactly 5:52 p.m. He tapped the watch with one shaking finger, met my eyes, rested his elbow on the chair, and waved to an invisible crowd. I could envision his shoulder leaning out the window of the locomotive; I could see the passengers on the platform waving back, through a bank of evaporating steam. I could see his lips were about to move, and they did.

His voice couldn't escape the dungeon where it had been chained for so many years. But with effort, he winked at me and clearly whispered, "King."

Dedicated to my Great Grandfather James Henry King, Engineer on the Pennsy for fifty-two years.

2. FALMOUTH WRECK

Photo Courtesy of Rehoboth Beach Historical Society and Museum

Shipwreck 1899

by Gary Hanna

Yards and yards of tangled
line keep the masts
from flying off in bitter wind.
Large sails are rolled
heavy across the deck,
extend beyond the ship
like arms reaching out
to balance a tilting world.
The *Falmouth* has run
aground, arrived too early
eager to reach the shore,
missed safe harbor,
welcoming dock at
journey's end. Gale force
winds and swirling rain
took control in the race
to reach her destination.
Now, she lists, helpless
on the beach, battered by
howling wind and mounting
wave, turned sideways,
falling over, too big
to be righted by man,
whose thought of taming
the ocean, snaps and groans,
and crashes, splintering
against the rock. Only pieces
will set it free, a reminder
for days to come.

The Wreck

by Bill Hicks

The remains of the storm continued to pound the beach just a few miles south of Rehoboth. In the gray mist of early morning she lay where they found her, washed up on the beach. Broken and battered, a few ropes entangling her and keeping her in the wash of the storm driven waves. A few of the locals were gathered in a tight knot, their voices barely heard over the crash of the surf. Her beauty was still evident, in spite of the damage wreaked by the howling nor'easter. Once again the Sea Witch had claimed another victim.

Twenty-four hours earlier, Will Kershaw had stood at the stern rail of the coastal schooner, the *Falmouth*, watching the low clouds scudding across the gray October sky. Building seas and a steady rain foretold of another nor'easter that they would have to face. The spindrift created a mist that sprayed the tops of the waves in gray sheets. Waves that were growing larger by the hour. The ship, running under reefed sails, was plowing through the ocean with white water washing across the deck as the bow slammed through the crests and sliced into the troughs.

Will pulled the oilskin coat tighter around him as the late October temperatures, combined with the spray of the waves, created a chill that ran bone deep into his body. He watched as his best friend, Jimmy Dugan, made his way across the lurching, tilting deck. They had signed on together hoping to make a life out of crewing on coastal schooners. Carrying cargo from Philadelphia to Charleston and back again was their most frequent run. Cotton, lumber, coal, and household goods were the constantly changing items stowed in the holds. As ordinary seamen, they furled and unfurled sails, handled the halyards and sheets, swabbed the decks, and raised and lowered the anchor, anything that required manual labor and brute force. The pay was good and the life exhilarating. It also got them out of one of the more squalid neighborhoods in Philadelphia.

Growing up on Leiper Street in the Frankford section of the city, Will and Jimmy had been neighbors and best friends. As they grew older their affection for each other grew as well, blossoming into a relationship that was closing in on forbidden territory. When they both ended their school careers at sixteen, they went to work in the Wingohocking Mills for a brief time. Longing for something better and more exciting, they signed on with the Bernardon Shipping Company, an old Philadelphia family that had been involved with ships for over fifty years. The company was always in search of young men to crew their ships, and Will and Jimmy fit the bill. Now both boys, just a few scant months past their eighteenth birthdays, found themselves bunkmates on The *Falmouth*, an old coastal schooner hanging on in this age of steam.

Jimmy huddled in close so his voice could be heard over the crash of the waves and the unceasing roar of the wind. "Will, this is looking like she's blowing up a pretty good gale."

"What's the matter? You a 'fraidy cat?" Will elbowed his friend in the ribs, but regretted it immediately, as he saw raw fear in his best friend's eyes. "Aw, c'mon, Jimmy, it'll be okay. This is just like the storm we hit off of Hatteras last March. Remember that one? Ice building on the shrouds and sheets, snow coming down, and wind that cut like a knife. We rode that one out just fine. Cap'n reefed the sails, and we barely slowed down. Nah, you don't have to worry, Jim, but if you do get too worried come and find me."

The *Falmouth* was off the coast of Maryland, somewhere north of Assateague Island, plowing slowly through the building seas, making only a slow three knots, sometimes not making way at all. Rain began falling harder and the winds picked up in speed and force. The man at the helm fought the big wheel as wind and current attempted to have their way with the 150 foot sailing ship. Waves began to regularly wash over the decks. Holding onto lifelines and any convenient handhold available, the two boys made their way to the companionway that led to the main salon below decks. They slid the hatch back and descended the ladder to the dimly lit cabin. Brass oil lamps, swinging wildly on their gimbals, valiantly tried to illuminate the dark area, but with all hatches closed, and no light coming through the deck prisms or ports, they were fighting a losing battle. Cuba Johnson, the cook, informed the sailors that the rough seas would not allow him to fire up the wood cook stove, so all meals would consist of bread, cheese, and some salt beef.

The noise of the storm was muffled below decks, but the sound of the ship straining against the wind and waves was amplified. Every joint creaked and groaned at the stresses being forced upon them. Any loose object rolled and banged against the deck and hull. Suspended objects created a mass of pendulums that swung in a crazy choreography that made the observer dizzy. Will and Jimmy joined some of the other crew at the long table where they would take their meals, play cards and dice games, or just sit and talk.

As they ate their breakfast of bread, cheese, and cold coffee left over from the night before, Jimmy's anxieties began to manifest themselves again. Each thump and groan caused him to look around for its source. Will, sensing his friend's growing fear, quietly moved his knee over and pressed it against the young man's leg. Jimmy cut his eyes to his friend at the sudden contact, even as this physical touch helped subdue his fear.

As the crew sat around the table, the talk gravitated to other storms that the old salts had weathered. August hurricanes in the West Indies, winter blizzards that froze boats in the harbors where they had sought refuge, and fall nor'easters that would consume a ship and not leave a trace. One man told of the Blizzard of '88. His ship, the *Paul and Johnson*, had sought refuge behind the Delaware Breakwater off of Lewes Beach, one of fifty or more vessels that had anchored behind the stone walls looking for relief from the hurricane force winds, blinding snow, and freezing temperatures. Another ship dragged its anchor, rammed the *Paul and Johnson*, and stove in her sides. Sinking quickly, the sailors made it safely to the ship that had rammed them, but that boat was eventually driven into the beach and lost as well. His tales of frozen men, sailors that had drowned, and close to thirty of those ships in the harbor that were destroyed, drove poor Jimmy nearly to tears. Will was quick to assess the situation and got his friend away from the grizzled sailors at the table before they could recognize Jimmy's fear and have an opportunity to tease the young sailor mercilessly. Jimmy had always been fragile emotionally. Quick with fears and quicker with tears. It was only through the efforts of his friend that he'd survived his adolescent years on Leiper Street. Time and time again, Will was able to intervene and absorb or deflect the cruelty that fourteen-year-old boys are capable of. Will was always sticking up for Jimmy when necessary, or making hasty departures when they were able. This was one of those times to leave.

"C'mon, Jimmy, I need some help securing some cargo down in the hold. Can you give me a hand?"

Walking through the passage and heading below to the cargo hold, Will almost pushed his friend along. Descending another ladder, the only light in the hold was the dim lamp that Will had lit. Crates, barrels, and other pieces of cargo were visible only as dark shadows. Away from the rest of the crew, and alone with Will, Jimmy succumbed to his fears and broke into sobs. Will took his friend into his arms and held him. His soothing words, and strong arms, gave the crying boy a sense of comfort and peace, and soon his tears ceased. They heard footsteps on the deck above them and quickly put some distance between themselves.

"Will, you are such a friend. I don't know how I would do this without you. I'm so afraid. It's all I can do to make myself look brave in the face of this storm."

"I'll never let you down. Now, wipe the snot off your face, and let's get back to the galley and finish that sumptuous feast we left when we had to 'secure this cargo.'"

Slowly inching her way up the coast, the *Falmouth* fought for every nautical mile gained. The storm intensified and the cargo ship found herself offshore of Rehoboth Beach, Delaware. Reaching the Breakwaters at Lewes was now out of the question, even though they lay only five miles to the north. The wind had reached a point where all the sails had to be lowered and the anchors dropped. A mile and a half offshore, the crew of the *Falmouth* made preparations to ride out the storm. The captain had two anchors lowered, both catching on the sandy bottom below, and was confident in his decision to lay-to and ride out the storm, at least until morning. Bobbing like a cork, the *Falmouth* was at the mercy of the wind, waves, tide, and currents, as she strained at her anchor lines.

Even though they were below in the main salon, the shrieking of the wind through the lines and shrouds reached the men's ears like a chorus of Harpies. The groan of the windlass was heard even over the wind. As the night and the storm wore on, the men retired to their bunks. The long hard sail up the Delmarva coast had been exhausting, but the sounds of the storm and the motion of the waves which kept the ship heaving and bucking as she tried to ride out the storm at anchor, left them knowing that their dreams would be fleeting.

Damp and cold, the thin mattress offering little comfort, Will Kershaw tried to sleep. The small cabin accommodated two sailors and was better than the old days when sailors slung hammocks below decks and all slept in the same area. Two bunks, two foot lockers and a small hanging locker made for tight quarters, but did offer a modicum of privacy.

Somewhere past eight bells, between midnight and 1:00 a.m., Will heard the sobs coming from the bunk of his best friend.

"Jimmy," he whispered, "C'mere. Climb in and bunk with me."

He heard shuffling in the dark cabin as his friend approached and squeezed into the tight bunk. Will wrapped his arms around him, and could feel the sobs that shuddered through his friend's body. After what seemed like hours, the silent crying diminished. Softly, Will kissed his friend's face. He could taste the salt of the tears and of the sea.

"Will, I can't do this anymore," Jimmy said. "I'm not cut out to be a sailor like you. I hate this life. I hate the sea. I hate living on this damp cold boat. When we get to Philadelphia, I'm done. I can get my job back at Wingohocking. I'd rather be a yarn monkey my entire life than make another voyage on this boat." With that, he started sobbing again. "Climbing the mast, crawling out on the sprit, even pissing over the rail, makes my heart pound, for I know that if I slip, if I fall, I'm dead. There will be no catching a rope or waiting for a rescue boat."

Rocking him and murmuring soft comforts, Will did his best to quell his friend's fears. He knew this would be their last voyage together. Perhaps the last time they would be together. Thoughts crashed through his mind as the waves crashed against the hull of the *Falmouth*. There were things he needed to say, to do, if this was the last time that they might be able to be this close. But to love another boy in 1899 was forbidden. Society, the church, the world, looked down upon them. Any intimacy between them could find them in prison. Ostracized. Fired from their jobs. Their families would shun and abandon them, and they would be left destitute and penniless on the streets of Frankford. With these thoughts reeling through his mind, and the motion of the ship, the promise of sleep became even more distant. He wasn't even sure how Jimmy felt. He thought he loved Jimmy. He wanted to love Jimmy, but there was so much that would work against them. Still, he vowed he would approach Jimmy once this storm had passed and see how his friend really felt. If there was a chance, maybe they would both leave the sea.

A report like that of a three-inch bow gun woke the entire crew around 6:00 a.m., followed by another sharp crack. Both anchor lines had parted due to the strain. The storm was at its peak and was now pushing the helpless ship so the waves were striking broadside instead of bow on. The *Falmouth* healed sharply to port as the waves and the wind pounded her starboard side. Men scrambled from their cabins to their stations topside. The ship's bell was being rung as an alarm. The captain was shouting orders barely heard above the roar of the winds and the incessant crash of the waves.

Will and Jimmy made it onto the deck and headed for the bow. The captain intended to raise a reefed staysail to try and get some type of steerage, so he could point his ship more into the wind. By doing so, he hoped she would be less vulnerable to the destructive winds and water. As they released the foresail halyard from the belaying pins in order to raise it, a monstrous wave broke over the starboard rail. Will was swept off his feet and washed toward the port side down the sloping deck. Jimmy watched in horror as his best friend was caught in the mass of water and foam and was being pushed toward the opposite rail.

Will had been taken by surprise as the wave crashed down upon him. The cold water knocked his feet from underneath him and sent him sliding across the deck. He still clutched the halyard and he hung on tightly. Riding the waves feet first down the tilting deck he was sure that his fate was sealed and he would be washed over the side. Blinking through the salt water, he saw Jimmy, mouth agape and eyes wide. If he was screaming, Will didn't hear it. His feet hit the toe rail and he felt the scrape of the wood against his shins.

As the remains of the wave washed over the side of the ship, Will clutched the line that he had just freed. His feet dangled over the side, but he was safe. He pulled himself fully onto the deck and got back on his feet. He forced a silly little grin and said to an ashen-faced Jimmy, "See, it's not so bad, Jimmy. Just make sure you have something to hold onto at all times."

His cavalier attitude belied the knowledge that he had been just inches from death and seconds from meeting his God. His heart pounded wildly in his chest. This was no time for personal fear though, and he and Jimmy worked with the other crewmen to get the foresail raised.

"Hey, Kershaw, you okay? You nearly took a Halloween swim there. You know the Sea Witch was down there waiting to kiss your pretty little face once you hit the water." Orien Abbot cast the first ribbing.

"Yeah, Willie, I hear the Sea Witch is sweet on young'uns like you." Mac McIntosh, one of the oldest crew members at forty-one, joined in the ribbing.

Will responded, "Mac, you're just jealous 'cause she would spit an old oyster like you right back on the deck."

The back and forth as the men worked to raise the sail helped ease the terror that was overtaking Jimmy, and helped Will's heartbeat return to something close to normal.

In spite of their efforts, the captain was unable to save his doomed ship. There just wasn't enough time and distance between them and the shoreline, nor water under her keel. Her first contact was no easy bump on the bottom. The waves slammed the foundering ship hard against the sand. Men were knocked to the deck, lines snapped, and items of cargo were heard shifting in the holds below. The next course of waves shoved the big ship further up on the beach. The crack of timbers and planking could be heard as once again she hit the beach.

Standing at the port rail the captain looked across thirty yards of roiling water to the dunes. A group of locals had gathered. If someone on shore was aware of the stranded ship, then the Lifesaving Station would be notified as well. There was no hope in lowering the long boat attached to the stern. The heavy seas would swamp it taking anyone in it to a watery grave. Perhaps, the captain had a chance to save his men even if he lost his ship.

The men on shore were within range of the ship's Lyle Gun; a thin, quarter inch line was fired from it and retrieved by them. A cheer went up on shore and ship when everyone saw that the plan would work. The crew of the *Falmouth* gathered at the rail in a knot and contemplated their next moves. Hanging from a rope thirty feet above the water and traversing one hundred feet to the dune would test the mettle of any man on a good day. To do it in the teeth of a nor'easter might be beyond their limits.

Mac was the first to go. "I'll see you on shore, boys, or I'll see you in Hell." He jumped up on the rail and started the long, perilous journey. Swinging like a monkey, he made the trip, dropped on the dry ground, and jumped up to wave to his crewmates back on board the broken schooner. Cuba the Cook was next to go, as one by one the men of the *Falmouth* saved themselves. Will and Jimmy looked at each other and knew that their turn had come. "Jimmy, you go first," Will told his friend. "I'll be right behind you. You can do this. Just hold tight and keep moving."

Jimmy reached up, grasped the thick line in his hands, and started to cross the water. He heard Will shouting encouragement from the deck of the listing ship. "One hand over the other. Don't look down. Keep it up, Jimmy. I'll be right behind you."

Unable to look back or see his friend, the sound of Will's voice spurred him on. He did look down momentarily. The water was a frenzied mass of breakers, foam, and spindrift. For a moment he froze there. His arms grew weak. His fingers ached. Then, faintly over the din of the storm he heard Will shouting to him, and he smiled, steeled his reserve, and started again.

Jimmy reached the dune and dropped to his knees exhausted and spent. He turned expecting to see Will close behind. Instead, he saw only the long stretch of line. Those still on board were leaning over the rail as if to see something in the water. With a wail Jimmy knew what they were searching for. He ran to the water's edge and scanned the foaming seas. He saw nothing. He saw no one. Alone standing in the wash, he screamed his friend's name. Crying out to the storm, to the Sea Witch, to the waves, over and over again. He fell to his knees in the wash and silently sobbed, "I loved him, but I couldn't tell him. He never knew. He'll never know."

The remains of the storm continued to pound the beach. In the gray mist, they found Will washed up, broken and battered, trailing lines entangling him and keeping him in the wash of the storm-driven waves. A few of the locals spotted him and waded out to retrieve the body; their voices barely heard over the crash of the surf. Once again the Sea Witch had claimed her prize.

Bad Weather Witch

by Crystal Heidel

"The blame will be on the Bad Weather Witch." Mrs. Marshall's voice dropped when she said witch. She picked up a jar of loose-leaf Earl Grey tea with lavender flowers from the shelf and placed it in one of the apothecary's shopping baskets.

Caroline Hudson knew what she meant.

When townspeople blamed the Bad Weather Witch, it was always doublespeak for another ship had wrecked.

From behind the check-out counter, Caroline stirred her tea and felt the prickling of apprehension sweep across her skin.

She'd spent years here in Southern Delaware making a life for herself and settling into a routine. Ten years ago, when she'd opened this general store, the Rose & Company Apothecary, she felt at home. She had been living in the proper town of Lewes in a beautiful home just a few minutes' walk from her store. It was an older style home, built in 1855 with brick and wood trim. It was simple, but she appreciated the fine craftsmanship and attention to detail both inside and out. No doubt in a hundred years, it would be considered historical—and she'd be around to see it. Maybe she'd even live in it again.

She loved her neighbors and her garden. She had friends she lunched with on a daily basis and a string of young, handsome lovers. She knew how to stay out of trouble by reading minds. It wasn't hard. Anyone could do it with enough time.

And she had always had time.

But this wreck down on Rehoboth Beach meant it was time for Caroline to move on again. The clock was ticking. It would only be a matter of time before someone found out the truth. Depression began to swell in Caroline's stomach like the water-filled mid-morning clouds hanging low in the sky. She cleared her throat. "Where?"

"The schooner *Falmouth* was anchored a mile and a half off shore." Mrs. Marshall turned her gaze on Caroline and for a moment, it was almost as if she knew Caroline's secret. "The storm must have snapped the cables. The *Falmouth* is on the beach. Past the high-water mark." She instructed her daughter to carry a five-pound bag of sugar to Caroline at the counter as she sadly shook her head. "It's a total loss. Mr. Marshall is down with other men helping with the rescue."

"So, there were no deaths?" Caroline held her breath.

Mrs. Marshall shook her head.

Caroline sighed with relief; at least the sailors were being rescued.

"Mother." The daughter nodded toward a small package of fine chocolates laced with lavender grown in Caroline's own backyard. Lavender was soothing and helped encourage sleep. "May we please get those?"

"Hush child. Your father shall be furious if I purchase that today. Perhaps next week."

That seemed to satisfy the girl, though Caroline wanted to give her the chocolates. It was clear she wasn't sleeping well. Caroline's magic-infused chocolate would help. But she'd learned long ago to not involve herself with family affairs. Those who needed help would seek her out. Caroline drew her attention to the items Mrs. Marshall was placing on the counter and mentally began to do the math. One jar of tea: 51 cents; the bag of sugar: 31 cents; a sun bonnet left over from summer: 30 cents; a jar of honey: 37 cents; two tins of Arnica Tooth Soap: 25 cents each; and a pound of coffee: 35 cents.

"Two dollars, thirty-four cent." Caroline began placing it all in a paper bag.

"Are you sure that's the total, Mrs. Hudson?"

At the use of her fake surname, Caroline paused, hand poised over the bag of sugar. She seemed to change identities so many times it was simply easier to choose names that wouldn't draw attention, names that were easier to remember and pronounce. And yet Hudson made her pause. Hudson was the name she used last time she lived here.

"I expected it to be more." Mrs. Marshall still stared.

Caroline smiled sweetly. "I discounted the hat since it was from summer."

Mrs. Marshall paid while her daughter beamed thanks, and then hurried for the door, muttering about wanting to go down to the beach to see the wreck.

The wreck. The word alone had Caroline's heart beating a bit faster. Blame will be on the Bad Weather Witch.

Caroline knew she had nothing to do with the schooner being cut loose from its mooring. But she couldn't help feeling it was her fault. After all, she was the cause of the storm. Her emotions always seemed to have an influence on the weather. She had never been able to learn to control it. When she was happy, it was sunny and calm, even in the dead of winter. When anger drove her, the wind was uncontrollable and storms brewed.

And last night she was both sad and angry at the same time. And those two emotions were a volatile combination: the storms were always ten-fold.

She knew that she had caused the storm last night, even if it wasn't intentional. And she knew that her emotions were the reason men were being rescued from a lost ship.

What added to the storm early this morning had been the day: All Hallows Eve.

Caroline gazed into her now cold black tea as she recalled the last time a storm brewed on All Hallows Eve off the shore of the Cape. But that storm she had purposely conjured and used to her advantage. Even now, she could feel the anger coursing through her. Anger at what had been happening to the people in her town. And anger at the person causing it all. On that night, the sky had darkened and the squalls of the ocean had nearly overturned the stolen boat as she rowed alone in the dark. The moon had been absent from sight, but strong; she had felt its power through the clouds and hammering rain.

In fact, she had been counting on its power.

She could hear his vicious oaths at her through the sealed, water-tight box. It amazed her how two people, at one time irrevocably in love, could use their knowledge of the other's emotions to inflict damage and pain. He had been just as cursed as she: to live an eternity. But his rage and unquenchable thirst for human blood had endangered them both. It had to be done. Not wanting his words to influence her as she worked her magic, she had flicked her wrist over the coffin, effectively silencing the sound from within. That moment was etched into her mind.

Now, standing in her apothecary, Caroline's throat tightened. She squeezed her eyes shut and reached for the amulet at her neck.

That last storm was one hundred and fourteen years ago.

Yes, she was the Bad Weather Witch.

And yes she was still alive.

And yes, she was still causing bad weather.

Caroline had been alive for millennia. Sometimes she forgot the exact year she'd been born, but other times it was crystal clear. Her history seemed to swim together, events and wars melting into one another—unless she was involved in them.

In August 1391 she'd watched as her friend Jeanne de Brigue, an accused sorceress, burned at the stake. She'd witnessed the freezing of the Seine in Paris in 1709 and the flooding and food riots that followed. She'd traveled by ocean and train and horse, walked along cobblestones in twelfth-century Greece and among the paved roads of New York City only twenty years ago.

Her name hadn't always been Caroline, and she hadn't always been alone. She used to travel with him until that fateful night in 1785.

Since then, she always moved away for a generation, and then returned, always creating a new identity. Always drawn back to him: to the man in the coffin at the bottom of the Delaware Bay.

Caroline decided to close the apothecary a little early. It felt like it had been days, but was only a scant five hours since Mrs. Marshall and her daughter had left. She checked the lock. Placing her hand on the glass, she thought, this could be the last night I close my shop.

She rushed home to change out of her floor-length rose colored day dress and into something more suited for the distance to Rehoboth Beach. Twisting her braided hair into a bun at the back of her head, she fastened it with pins. She tightened the dark blue wool coat around her, buttoning it from her chest to her waist. It flared out from there, its tail covering her equally dark blue wool dress.

Rehoboth was nearly eight miles away and the temperature had dropped as the sun began to do the same.

The clock read 4:35. She sighed.

By the time she found a horse and cart headed that way and arrived at the wreck, it would be well after six. There wouldn't be enough daylight to see the ship. Even now it was getting dark.

But why did she want to see the wreck so badly? What was it that compelled her to see it? Caroline's fingers moved to her amulet again. Could it be that she'd buried a monster and she wanted to make sure it was still buried?

Instead of dwelling on why, she concentrated on how to get there. She turned her attention to her indoor garden, eyeing the mint and mugwort. She felt her mouth twitch and smiled. She supposed she'd travel the old-fashioned way.

Caroline didn't waste a moment pinching off herbs she needed and set to work at her altar, placing them in a mortar and beginning to crush them. She added a sprinkle of vervain and yarrow, lit a white candle and poured hot water into the mortar. The spell was simple. She'd cast it hundreds of times before the age of thirteen.

She lifted the stone cup to her lips and drank. In her mind she pictured the ocean and sand, imagining she would end up under the boardwalk around Surf Avenue. If she recalled correctly, there would be enough room under the boards there to stand. She swallowed the contents of the mortar: water and herbs and then let the ancient words flow from her tongue, melting into the air that was now sparkling, turning shades of grey and white and pale green and blue. The room began to move. The doors seemed to breathe and the windows warped, as if bending in and over themselves. Inhaling softly, she said the final word and closed her eyes, then waited for the spinning to cease.

When it did, she opened her eyes and felt the cold breath of salt air on her face. The wind hadn't yet died down and the sound of rushing waves coursed around her.

Caroline would never tire of that feeling of traveling by witchcraft. The sensation of being weightless, seeing the strings that bind the Universe together. Using them as a guide to get from one place to another.

The embers of her magic dissipated. She emerged from below the boardwalk and glanced around, hoping no one had seen the shimmer-light display under the boards. Relief flooded her as she realized that all eyes were on the *Falmouth* wreck up the beach.

Up on the boardwalk, she made her way quickly toward the wreck. With every step, the wooden boards creaked, sending a sliver of dread up her spine. Marshall and her daughter. They must have left the Rose & Company this morning and straightaway headed to Rehoboth. The Lyons and Carters. Caroline nodded hello to others whose names escaped. Her focus was the wreck.

How had the moorings and cables snapped? How many men were aboard the ship? Was it truly a loss? How bad had the storm been to send it over the high-water mark and onto the sandy beach, listing toward the ocean, as if desperate to get back out to sea. The sails had been lowered, and a rope was tied from the mast and staked inland.

Waves crashed along the outer hull of the ship, eroding the sand, sending it further leaning toward the ocean like a child's toy in the mud.

The crowds had begun to dissipate and Caroline was able to find a place to lean against the railing at the boardwalk. She was a few dozen yards down from Horn's Pavilion. Last night the winds had driven the boat a mile and half inland. Caroline's gaze swept out past the *Falmouth*, out as far as her eyes could see: the ocean was calmer; the line between sky and sea now visible. The waves on the shore were hardly larger than normal, but still rushed around the boat.

That's when she spotted them. Two men. Just about six feet above the word FALMOUTH on the stern of the ship a man sat on the railing, his feet thrown over the edge, facing the shore and holding onto the dingy that had never been launched, as if he were about to leap to the sand below. She held her breath and waited. But he only sat there, conversing with the other man, standing a few yards away.

The rescue line was attached to the mizzen mast, the mast closest to the stern. Another wave crashed around the hull and she imagined the storm last night, the storm she created from her tumultuous emotions. Something had to be done.

Caroline turned away, unable to continue to look at the ship she had wrecked.

"Bad Weather Witch," a man's indignant slur cut through the air as he held his wife's arm and began walking her back toward Horn's Pavilion.

Caroline stared after them, unable to tear her gaze away, but wanting to dispel the slanderous name. She was the Bad Weather Witch.

But if people knew, would they understand?

She needed to get back home. She needed to move. She needed to leave Delaware.

It was time to move on.

Depth Finder

by Wendy Elizabeth Ingersoll

Tall ships tack up the inlet as I consider
the skeleton on our tourboat's sonar
just off Long Neck, shadow settled
on an ancient sandbar, wreckage
mimicking itself as well as bay bed.
    Our captain tells the tale:
two hundred years ago, commercial schooner at anchor,
sailors resealing deck seams with bubbling tar, a spark,
the tar ignites, flames unfurl full tilt,
envelop the cargo of staves, the ship lists, rolls,
sinks like gloaming sun's implode.
    One of our party gasps, wrings her hands.
Slaves, she moans,
the slaves all burned.
    Staves, our captain barks, staves for making
barrels.
    I lurch back from the sonar screen,
reach for the rail, quivering from my wavery glimpse—
        among the schooner's ribs and backbone
        resting in inlet's crypt:
        smaller bones and limbs
        half-buried in the sand.

3. MAN WITH CRAB NET

Photo Courtesy of Rehoboth Beach Historical Society and Museum

The Crab Pot

by Mary Pauer

Preparations for crabbing with Grandma began before we decapitated a chicken for bait.

First, we plunged into the darkness of the back shed; its humidity clung to my eyelashes. While I blinked, Grandma headed to a shelf for the bushel-basket stained with salt water, the slats bleached white like ocean spume. "Take this," she said, handing me the basket.

Inside, like skeins of wool to knit, sat white string lines, nestled on old rags. Between sat hooks, lead sinkers of pyramidal and rectangular shapes, and a knife with a long blade.

I balanced the basket on my hip. "And the net?"

Grandma reached overhead. The pole holding a woven cotton net rested on two nails, waiting for us to carry, like Tom Sawyer on an adventure. I toted the basket and she, the net. After the dimness of the shed, the bright light stunned, almost blinded me. I was glad, for I hated the next step, but I would never give up the chance to be with Grandma.

A short-handled hatchet balanced in the cracks of a tree stump. Moving near the garden, Grandma clucked, "Here chick-chick," clicking her fingers as if to offer a treat. Unsuspecting, a hen approached.

As quick as I could turn my head away, Gram grabbed its feet, held it to her chest. As much as I loved crabbing, the flapping and the alarmed squawk of the bird terrified me. She twisted the neck.

She lay the newly dead chicken on the stump. "You can help now."

I held the still twitching feathered body with my hands and closed my eyes. I heard the thump of the axe and the crinkle of bones separating like a plate breaking.

"Done." She lifted my hand away, patted it. "Good."

She hung the chicken to drain. Tomorrow, the carcass for soup; later, the feathers claimed for pillow stuffing.

Today, we used the neck as bait. According to her, the juiciest crabs preferred "chicken necks, the fresher the better."

The wooden bridge where we crabbed hung over a tidal creek that swished onward to the ocean. Before we climbed up, I waded into shallow water to wet the rags that would cover and cool our catch.

Grandma set up in the middle of the bridge, as she preferred the faster and deeper water underneath, although the creek was shallow enough to see ripples at the bottom.

Setting crab lines is a complex process. First, hooks are attached to the end of the twine. Then a small knot holds the sinker to weigh the lines, heavy enough to find the sandy bottom, yet alive enough to flow with the current, to entice the crabs to nibble.

We used the bridge planks as our cutting board. I swatted flies as she chopped the neck into smaller bits and finally, she threaded the chunks onto the barbed hooks.

Then we were ready to lower our lines. We did not use bobbers, rather, we stared into the translucent liquid until a dark shadow floated near, like an underwater cloud, and reached to taste the meat.

"Do not move." She placed her hand on my shoulder. "If they sense a shadow, they'll scuttle away."

Grandma knew if I pulled up too fast I'd have an empty line. If I waited too long, crabs snatched the bait away, and I'd have an empty line. An adept crabber used the same neck joint, hour after hour, rarely losing meat to the hungry hard-shelled crabs.

My job was to raise the line while she netted the crab, scooping and tossing it into the basket with a flick of her wrist. After the first minutes of searching, I shut my eyes against the hypnotic motion of the water below.

When I missed hauling up a line, Grandma tssked. Then she worked the line herself with one hand, capturing the crab in the net with her other. "You'll get better."

She never let the crabs sit in the basket for too long, and we never took more than we needed: half a bushel, sufficient for dinner that night. By then the basket was alive with the hiss of popping bubbles, a sound I loved.

I peeked under the cloths to watch them pinch each other, their wiry antennae swaying, bulbous eyes staring but not blinking, each claw scraping and snapping. "Why is one claw bigger?"

"It's the hunting pincer."

As soon as the flesh on our chicken neck vanished, Grandma untied the sinkers and hooks. She rolled the lines, tossed the bones into the creek. They rose in the current, tiny puzzle pieces floating to sea.

We laid everything on top of the cloth, and carried the heavy, awkward basket between us, one handle in her hand, one in mine.

In the garden, we upended the basket into a metal bucket. Claws scrabbled on the sides. I pushed with the pole end of the net. "Stay there," I told them.

In the kitchen she filled the cooking pot with water, green basil, fresh oregano, garlic bulbs, and an entire banana pepper. A dash of paprika and several slices of red onion completed the mixture. She covered the pot.

While we waited for the water to come to a hard boil, which seemed to take forever, I asked, "Did you do this when you were a kid?"

Grandma said, "Wash your hands and sit at the table." She reached to the top of the breakfront for a book with black pages. She wiped nonexistent dust from the pebbled cover with her apron.

I knew, but said, "Your photograph album."

She pulled her chair closer to mine. "My mother's." Her hair tickled my cheek. I smelled the brackish odor on our skin and tried to wait as patiently as she had taught me for crabbing. Still I kicked at the legs of the chair.

Gram opened the book. "Careful, don't rip the pages."

I rose to my knees on the seat to study the mounted photographs. Some were warped, others torn and yellowed. Faded black and white prints showed indistinct faces that could have belonged to anyone. I was disappointed with the frozen pictures but I wouldn't say so. I would have hurt her feelings.

Grandma turned to the second page where I saw a photograph of men standing on a pier.

I think she sensed my dissatisfaction. "Look." She pointed to a man in the foreground, his head cocked at a jaunty angle, a smile on his face. Across his body, between him and the camera, he held a crabbing net.

I pressed my slightly damp finger onto the corner. "Who's he?"

Grandma pulled my hand from the page, pushed the album away and did not speak.

"Gram?"

"My father."

"Did he teach you to crab?"

"No."

I saw the date written at the bottom of the photo, 1897, and noticed another man in the background, wearing a white sailor uniform. An American flag hung at the end of the dock, listless, on what must have been a still day. "How come?"

"How come what?"

"He didn't go crabbing with you?"

"He went to sea."

"After that did he?"

"Did he what?"

"Teach you to crab."

"He died before I was born."

I lay my head on her shoulder. "You didn't know him?"

"He sailed to Cuba on a ship called the Maine."

"Did he get sick?"

"The ship blew up...in the harbor."

I felt her steady breath, yet pressed against her more closely. "Did you love him?"

"He was my father."

The pot lid on the stove rattled. Herbed steam escaped, filling the room with aromatic scents.

"It's ready." Gram stroked my hair, closed the album before I could ask who taught her to crab. "Come now."

Together we went to the garden for the crabs, then hoisted the bucket over the hot broth. Crabs tumbled in, twisting as their bodies turned to escape, quickly changing from mottled green to silent pink. The boiling foam curled with flecks of spices and bits of shell.

I wondered if she missed her father.

4. FRIENDS

Photo Courtesy of Rehoboth Beach Historical Society and Museum

A Golden Day on the Boardwalk
with Grandma and the Great Aunts

by Irene Fick

I knew them only as middle-aged or old women in matronly housedresses, preoccupied with cooking, cleaning and other household chores. So, when my cousin cleaned out her attic and mailed me this century-old photo, I was startled—yet charmed. The image was a teaser; reminding me how little I actually knew about my Italian ancestors and making me want to learn more.

It is 1916 in the photo. In front, waving and looking uncharacteristically confident is Grandma Antonia, known as the shy, reserved sister. She was nineteen then. To her left, Great Aunt Rosalie—considered the pretty, bubbly sister—holds a dark parasol. On the right is Great Aunt Francesca—known as "Tall Fannie" because at five foot three she towered over her sisters, and almost everyone else in the clan. Behind the sisters is their unassuming brother, Great Uncle Guido, with his trademark pompadour, bushy eyebrows and dashing good looks that attracted so many young ladies.

These dark-eyed beauties are relishing a flawless sunny day in Rehoboth Beach as they mug for the camera. The women are wearing soft, shapely white chiffon dresses, and Guido sports a white shirt, and most likely, matching white trousers.

Grandma, the Great Aunts and Uncle Guido lived in Wilmington's Little Italy, then known as "The Hill." It was home to many immigrants from southern Italy's peasant villages who settled there between 1880 and 1920. On the day the photo was taken, I suppose they came to Rehoboth to visit friends, or, perhaps simply to explore the resort community. They may have traveled by train (on the Delaware Railroad) or Uncle Guido could have borrowed a new Ford Model-T sedan from a prosperous buddy.

Grandma was just thirteen when she and her family joined the infamous "huddled masses" and crossed the Atlantic in 1910. Like so many others with little or no income, they were crammed into the dark, noisy and smelly steerage area of the ship. There they remained for more than a week until they sailed into New York Harbor and were greeted by the Statue of Liberty; that mighty woman with the big torch. I'm not certain how long they remained in New York, but the family ultimately settled in Delaware, perhaps to pursue opportunities for work on the railroads or in the building trades.

A few years after this photo was taken, in 1919, Grandma Antonia met and married Grandpa Salvatore, who had also come to the United States from Italy. Grandma gave birth to five daughters (one was my mother), but miscarried her sixth child, the coveted boy that Grandpa so dearly wanted. The family remained in Little Italy, purchasing a two-story row house.

Great Aunts Fannie and Rosalie and Uncle Guido also married and had children. Aunt Fannie lived in the upstairs flat, while Aunt Rosalie moved down the block. Uncle Guido (who died in the 1943 influenza epidemic) lived around the corner.

All of their children remained close. Most stayed in Little Italy, moving into row houses with small front porches and tiny lawns, most blessed by statues of the Virgin Mary (and a pink flamingo for a dash of color). Their homes, we once joked, were in "shouting distance" of each other. Only a few of the children moved away, but even they did not go too far afield. Those adventurous families settled into split-levels or ranch homes in the middle-class suburbs north of Wilmington.

My immediate family was different. We were the outliers. Dad, Mom, my brother and I left Wilmington in the early 1950s for the Chicago suburbs, where Dad found white-collar work in the insurance industry. Truth is, he wanted to escape the proximity and interference of the extended family. He used to say that my mother's family came attached to his wedding ring. We carved out an independent life in a white-bread suburb with curved streets named after Indian tribes, large fenced backyards and hardly any noise.

I don't think my mother's family ever forgave Dad for "taking us away." They did tend to hold grudges. The only other renegade was a cousin who relocated to central Jersey when she married. Quite a ruckus ensued over that move.

With the exception of phone calls and letters, our only link with the larger family was our annual 750-mile road trip to Wilmington for summer "vacation" where we would stay with family members. After a week or so, Dad would go back to his Chicago job. At summer's end, he returned to take us home.

The memory of those summer visits remains strong and vivid. When our Chevy sidled to the curb of Grandma Antonia's house, she would crush me and my brother to her housedress; cry out in her broken English how tall we had grown, yet how skinny we were (skin and bones she would say). She would then give us her loose change for ice cream at the corner store.

What I most cherished, however, were the summer day trips to Rehoboth Beach. Grandma and the Great Aunts would remain at home, doing what they did best: cooking, cleaning, tending to their houses. My brother and I relied on the next generation—our aunts and uncles (and cousins)—to carry on the family tradition of sunning at the seashore. These beach days always included strolls on the boardwalk, cotton candy, pizza, fries and ice cream, but what we enjoyed most was simply digging deep into the sand, building castles, taking tentative dips into the ocean.

Another highlight of those summer visits was the elaborate Sunday dinner. We would gather at noon in Grandma's dining room for a meal that went on for several hours. The food was always some variation of pasta (lasagna, ravioli, spaghetti, ziti), meatballs or sausage, bread, and salad (iceberg lettuce and tomatoes dressed with oil and vinegar). The table was a free-for-all battleground where elbows collided as grandparents, aunts, uncles and cousins reached for second and third helpings. There was no such thing as polite dinner conversation (how was your day?) just the sounds of passionate eating—chewing, chomping, slurping and the occasional shout to pass this or that dish.

After dinner, we kids would play outside while the adults sipped coffee and relaxed in the living room, resting on sofas and chairs embalmed in plastic and surrounded by cabinets and end tables lined with porcelain bric-a-brac. In the early evening, we were called back to the dining table for more: cold cuts, cheeses, sweets. (Later on, I understood why no one in my extended family was considered slim.)

Perhaps the housedresses are what I most recall about Grandma and the Great Aunts—in fact, the only times they did not wear their housedresses were on special occasions like weddings, baptisms or funerals, or their occasional visit to Sunday Mass.

The housedresses suited their by-now bulbous bodies and were ideal for cleaning, laundry, cooking. Made of cotton, they had oversized pockets and fussy patterns that included olive trees or plump purple grapes or sheep grazing the verdant fields of Italy. Always, they were scented with garlic, onions, cooking oil and red sauce—sauce that had been simmering on the stovetop for hours and hours.

Grandma and the Great Aunts (and Grandpa Salvatore and Great Uncle Guido) have long since died. Ironically, they all passed away during the 1980s, in their nineties. They had what we might now consider "easy" deaths...they did not endure long, debilitating illnesses, months or years in and out of hospitals or nursing homes. Their minds remained intact. Some died suddenly at home, others after spending just a brief time in a local hospital.

During those long summer visits, it never occurred to me to ask Grandma and the Great Aunts about their lives and their rich histories. Like many young people, I was mired in the cocoon and conceit of youth. Grandma and the Great Aunts were background, not terribly interesting. Back then, I saw them as fleshy middle-aged or old women in housedresses, women with ordinary lives, harboring ordinary wisdom, women who remained in the tight circles of their large, loving families. That was enough.

Now, however, when I study this photo, this unexpected gift to memory, I see young people brimming with vitality and I know they were so much more than their housedresses. Facing the camera, on that glorious day at the beach in Rehoboth, they are eternally young, eternally free.

The Ocean Virgins

by Jessica Gordon

Mae.

We met in New York as children, that blazing hot July day in 1901 when I noticed her on Beekman Avenue. As I stood in the shade of the market's awning waiting for my mother to emerge with the groceries, she appeared from around the corner. While I noticed most children my age, she was unlike any other nine year old I had ever seen. Her dress was made of layer upon layer of ruffles, so white it almost hurt my eyes. Her hair was pulled up in a perfectly round, tight bun, and she walked so tall and with such grace, I felt I was watching a moving statue.

I don't know what she saw in me—my dirty, torn clothes? My unkempt hair? She marched right up to me and introduced herself. I can't remember what we talked about, but I liked her immediately. To my surprise, the feeling seemed mutual. The next time I went to town with my folks, she strode over to me again. "Greta! Have you ever played hopscotch?"

We had nothing in common that I could see, besides the fact that we were both girls of similar ages. Her family was wealthy, a well-known name in the Hudson Valley. My parents had emigrated from Germany just before I was born with little more than the clothes on their backs. People knew us as, "That Family with Seven Kids Who Live on the Old Raeburn Farm."

Mae spoke with confidence, looked people (even adults!) in the eye, asked questions and was never afraid to try something new. I hardly spoke, and when I did, my voice was barely audible. I definitely didn't look people in the eye, (certainly not adults!), and I regarded new things as foreign and therefore frightening.

But Mae challenged me. She asked about my dreams, suggested I come up with some, and spurred me to go after the ones I did. Like learning to read. Mae introduced me to the alphabet not long after our market meeting. She helped me string letters together, sat with me under the endless oaks in her yard while I slowly, excruciatingly sounded out words and stumbled through sentences. By the time we were twelve, I was reading about Sherlock Holmes and the March sisters and traveling to places in my mind I never knew existed.

She encouraged me to keep speaking German, because "It's your native language, darling, and how fabulous to be able to speak two languages!"

Being friends with Mae was exciting. I saw her as the sun: everyone wanted to be in Mae's rays, wrapped up in her enthusiasm and energy. I couldn't fathom what she got out of being friends with me.

Still, we always had fun together. Whether swimming in the lake (guess who taught me to swim?) or reading together (Mae's family library was massive), it seemed there was always something to giggle about.

Even now I can hear her laughing, see the arc of her throat as she tossed back her head of black curls, eyes closed, mouth open, her impossibly white, perfectly straight teeth on display. It was the kind of laugh that drew you in, made you smile, and want to know more about her.

Indeed, Mae's friends referred to her laugh as "The Lasso."

"I wasn't going to [insert ridiculously ludicrous act/event/idea here], but then she threw that lasso out, and I had no choice," they would say, grinning sheepishly.

One morning as I hung clothes on our line in the yard, Mae appeared suddenly, as she always did, as if she rode the wind everywhere she went.

"Greta, darling," she called as she half walked, half skipped over to me. And then, "Have you ever seen the ocean?"

Mae was always up to something, but you never knew what until you were smack dab in the middle of it.

"The ocean?" I asked, knowing sometimes answering with a question was more prudent than giving an actual answer.

"Yes. The ocean," she said, hands on her hips. "You know, that big, blue mass of liquid called the Atlantic?" she teased, daring me to answer with another question. "Have you ever seen it?"

I hadn't. Despite growing up not very far from it, I had never in my eighteen years of life set eyes upon the ocean. This fact had never bothered me, and it had never occurred to me that it should.

Mae knew my answer before she asked the question. Nodding emphatically, she declared, "Just as I thought."

As she danced towards my house, she called over her shoulder, "Pack your bags, darling. I'll speak with your parents."

Now, any normal person asking my parents for permission to take me on a trip to the beach wouldn't have the slightest chance of getting a "yes." There were countless reasons I couldn't go—cows to be milked, chickens to be fed, clothes to be washed and hung and six younger siblings to take care of, to name a few—and in my parents' opinion, it was frivolous to travel anywhere. They saw no point to it, no reason to leave our farm, our town. We were a content family, not wanting or needing much more than we already had. Any normal person would have been laughed, scolded even, right out our front door.

But Mae wasn't any normal person.

Somehow she convinced my parents to let me join her. I wish I could have heard what she'd said, seen how she flipped her hair and batted her infinite eyelashes, speaking—in that husky, velvety voice—of what I would see and learn and experience, so that even my parents would have wanted to join us.

Of course she would have mentioned that everything would be taken care of, naturally. Finally, she would have thrown out The Lasso, so that by the time she was done my parents nearly packed my bag for me.

I could hardly believe it, but one minute I was hanging diapers and the next I was on my way to a state called Delaware, hours from where I'd spent my entire life. I had never been away from home, and now I was spending three nights with a friend in an unfamiliar place on the ocean.

I was only slightly disappointed to learn that she had asked two other "Ocean Virgins" as Mae called us to come along as well, but was too excited to care too much about sharing Mae with Ruth Benson and Chester Graham. I didn't really know either of them, but I did know I was the baby of the group, the opposite role I was used to playing in my family.

I could tell I had company in the excited-but-anxious department; Ruth twirled her hair incessantly and seemed to hold her breath over every body of water we crossed, and Chester's nervous laughter followed nearly every sentence of Mae's.

When we crossed the state line from New Jersey into Delaware, Mae broke into song. "We've made it! The first time in the First State for all of you, how wonderful!" she boomed, clapping and whooping and making us all chuckle. For once Ruth stopped twirling and Chester's laugh was genuine. I felt myself relax a little more.

As we drove further south, I began to notice the aroma. It was an alien scent but one I instinctively knew was the ocean. And then Mae's driver announced our arrival. The sun was going down, but Mae insisted we had time for "a dip."

The air felt lush, as if tiny, invisible droplets were dancing all around me, some sticking to my skin. The setting sun was still warm on my back as we walked toward the sand, but goosebumps of anticipation covered my flesh.

I could hear it. The rhythmic roar of its waves, the sound of it crashing into the shore. My stomach started jumping around the closer we got; the louder the roar, the more jumping.

Mae ordered our shoes off when our feet hit the sand. Warm and grainy, it was different from the sand near the lake at home; finer, lighter, tacky.

As we headed up the hill of sand ("These are dunes," Mae told us), I kept my eyes forward, unblinking, not wanting to miss the exact moment I met this enormous, miraculous, living thing I had lived so close to but was completely unacquainted with.

Suddenly instead of beige-brown dune and blue sky, I saw another layer, in between dune and sky, dark blue, electric, alive. I was almost running now, the rush of water louder and louder in my ears, and as I reached the top of the dune I remember taking in a long, deep gasp.

It was endless. Where it met the sky there was an impossibly thin, straight line. The tiny droplets in the air danced all over my skin now, the smell of ocean throughout my nostrils, the sound of waves taking over all other noise in my ears, aside from my rapid heartbeat.

Mae stood with her back to the ocean, observing the reactions of the Ocean Virgins with a smile that nearly took up her entire face. I can imagine Ruth, Chester and me standing there, mouths agape, Mae more interested in us than what we had traveled to see.

"Hahaaaaaaaaaa!!" she hooted, dancing in the sand, arms in the air. "Isn't it beautiful?"

We were speechless.

None of the books I'd read prepared me for the vastness of the Atlantic, the white crests of the waves, the way they came to an apex, crumbled, then slid onto the sand, beckoning those with only toes in the water, then pulling back, inviting the toes to come in further.

"C'mon!" Mae shrieked as she ran toward the water. Naturally we ran after her, then came to a screeching halt at the shoreline. Mae was already wading in, beautiful clothes be damned, reporting on the perfect temperature of the water, how she could see her feet, that she thought she saw a fish.

Chester looked at his clothes—not half as nice as Mae's—and threw practicality into the wind, running in after Mae fully clothed, screaming in delight.

Ruth and I looked at each other. I knew how to swim, and was confident Mae wouldn't have brought Ruth along if she wasn't a swimmer as well. But this was no lake. The sheer delight in the voices we heard coming from the ocean was baiting, but I was scared, and from the look on her face, so was Ruth.

And then this girl I hardly knew held her hand out to me. A small smile and determined look gave me some kind of confidence I hadn't known before that moment. We would do this together. I took a deep breath, looking right into Ruth's eyes, and grabbed her hand.

Squealing with terror and exhilaration, we ran for the Atlantic. The cool rush of water hit my calves, thighs, stomach, shoulders, the crown of my head. I tasted the salt, felt my heart pounding in my chest and ears, and came to the surface smiling. I threw my arms around her then, marvelous, magical, magnanimous Mae.

We spent our time in Rehoboth in the water, barely getting out to eat and sleep. We swam, dove, splashed, rode wave after wave into the shore and floated with our faces to the sun. On land we marveled over the water webs that formed on our fingers and toes, the dark shades of our skin, the sticky film of salt water and sand on our bodies.

At night we ate in elegant restaurants. Our hotel, overlooking the ocean, was as magnificent as Mae's house, but bigger. The fact that as Mae's Ocean Virgins we wouldn't have cared where we stayed or what we ate was of no consequence to her. She loved to share what she had, but more than that, she loved to share what she loved.

Ruth, Chester and I became fast friends. We kept an eye on one another in the water, warned of fish or crabs that came our way, and laughed. Lord, did we laugh. I remember having sore cheeks and thinking I had never laughed so much in my life, not in eighteen years of laughter put together.

Our last day in Rehoboth, we returned to our rooms to find Mae had laid out outfits for each of us, clothes and accessories she'd brought from home. Gorgeous white dresses for Ruth and me with matching sunglasses and headbands, jewelry and parasols, and a crisp white shirt and trousers for Chester.

We didn't ask any questions as we got dressed, smiles on all of our faces as we knew whatever Mae had planned for us would be good.

Emerging from our rooms, we presented ourselves to Mae. She assessed each of us, tweaking a collar here, tightening a sash there. Finally, she stood before us, as she had when we first met the ocean, a satisfied grin on her face.

"We're ready," she declared, and led us outside to the wooden boards where her driver met us. I had heard of the contraption he held in his hands, but had never seen one.

"Ladies and gentleman," Mae announced, "We are going to take a photograph."

Chester in the back, Ruth at Mae's right side, me at her left. I remember feeling so proud, so fortunate, to have my photograph taken in Mae's clothes, on the boards overlooking my new friend: the ocean; surrounded by three more friends, two of whom I had met only days before.

Just as Mae's driver took the picture, she half waved, half saluted the Atlantic.

"Good-bye, Rehoboth, darling," she called as we headed to her car. "Until next time!"

On our ride home, as Ruth and Chester slept, I tried to figure out how I could possibly thank Mae for a trip that changed my life. As I uttered her name, all words seemed to vanish from my vocabulary. All I managed was, "I'm so happy I'm no longer an Ocean Virgin." With that, Mae's smile grew until it almost touched her ears. And then, as she relaxed into her seat and closed her eyes, she said, "Greta, darling, you ain't seen nothing yet."

The Unraveling

by Rita Nelson

Susan gently took the yellowed photograph from Peggy's withered hand. It was a photo of three young women and a man standing on the Rehoboth boardwalk. Susan turned it over to see if anything had been written on the back and was stunned by what she read. Staring at the words for what seemed like an eternity, she eventually realized her first priority was her mother's Aunt Peggy, and she slipped the photo into her pocket. She'd just have to sort this out later, she thought.

She pulled the purple, floral print flannel blanket over Peggy's frail body, tucking it in around her shoulders and making sure her feet were covered. Purple was always Peggy's favorite color. She poured a glass of water from the pitcher of ice water on the nearby nightstand, dipped a large cotton swab in it, and dabbed it on Peggy's parched lips. It wouldn't be long now. Susan got up and adjusted the Venetian blinds so that the sun no longer fell on Peggy's closed eyes.

Tears coursed down Susan's cheeks as she sat next to Peggy's bed and remembered the healthy, vibrant aunt she knew in her youth. Peggy was the belle of any ball, the life of the party, that person everyone wanted to have as a friend. She had never married, saying it just wasn't her cup of tea. She retained her youthful figure well into her eighties. Her wit and charm never left her, and even up to a week ago she had joked about how she would get a card from the

President when she reached her hundredth birthday. She'd even commented on how handsome her nurse was, and if she were younger, she'd be chasing him down the hall. Her birthday was yesterday when she turned ninety-six, but Peggy was not well enough to celebrate. It was May 24, 1994, the same birth date as Queen Victoria, a monarch Peggy greatly admired. She said it was Victoria who instilled a sense of morality and manners in the free world.

Susan, an only child, was raised by her Great Aunt Peggy from the time she was four after her father died from war injuries in 1948 and her mother, bereft beyond recovery, committed suicide. Susan didn't remember much about her parents and Peggy would only say they were a lovely couple who had come to a tragic end. Peggy kept a picture of them on the Duncan Phyfe drum table in the living room of her modest Victorian house in Millsboro, Delaware, a house she inherited from her parents and the house where she was born. Peggy had been a warm, engaging, yet strict mother to Susan, and through the years they became more like mother and daughter, than niece and aunt.

Each summer Peggy rented a small two-bedroom cottage in Rehoboth Beach in the first block from the ocean. It was a tradition her own parents had begun in 1908. Although her teacher's salary was not large, Peggy managed to save enough each year for this luxury. She would move there with Susan at the end of the school year in June and stay until after Labor Day. Peggy had a small circle of close friends at the beach. She walked the boardwalk in the late afternoon so she wouldn't burn her porcelain skin. She liked to read in the mornings over breakfast, and often met friends for lunch or a friendly game of whist. Her wild days were more or less behind her, but her charm never faltered. Summer dinners were on the front porch of the cottage, or at a local restaurant on the boardwalk. Susan and her friends had tea and card parties, played on the beach, built sandcastles, ate ice cream and salt water taffy. As Susan grew older, she flirted with the young lifeguards, hoping one would pay some attention to her. They rarely did.

Susan moved from the bedside to the reclining chair in Peggy's room, pulled a throw over her lap and closed her eyes. Sitting vigil with Peggy was the least she could do for the woman who raised her, gave her the depth of moral values, listened to her teenage whining, and stood firm and fast through those tumultuous teenage years and beyond. It was Peggy who walked her down the aisle when she married Thomas, and Peggy who held her hand through the pain of two births. It was always Peggy who stood on her side of any issue, and it was Peggy who never wavered in her devotion to Susan. Peggy was Susan's rock. Now it was Susan's time to be Peggy's rock and see her through to the end.

As Susan's eyes teared up, she reached into her pocket for a tissue and brushed the ragged edge of the photo. She took it out and looked deeply into the eyes of the young women. The one in the middle she knew was Peggy. Susan ran her finger slowly over the face of her aunt, tracing her slender nose, her large, bright eyes, and her infectious smile. In a rather primitive hand, "Rehoboth 1916" was scribbled on the front. Turning the photo over, it was dated Sunday, July 17. It was a happy photo, except for the young man who seemed a bit foreboding as he stood in the back. It was this man who intrigued Susan. The note in Peggy's handwriting read:

Me with my sister Dottie on my right, and friend Helen on my left and James who married Helen in September 1919. He was the love of my life and the father of my son born in June 1917, given up for adoption.

Nothing more.

Susan held her head in her hands. She was shocked to learn Aunt Peggy had a child, given up for adoption in 1917. He would be 77 now. She wondered if he was still alive, who he was, where he lived. There was never any family lore about him and Susan's genealogy work never turned up any evidence of a baby born out of wedlock and given up for adoption. She wondered if her recent DNA test would have revealed any such connection. Susan hadn't paid much attention to the results, but now, with this new information, she thought she had better take a closer look. He would be her mother's first cousin and her first cousin once removed.

Aunt Peggy moaned softly and waved her right hand in the air as if to summon Susan. The movement broke Susan's focus on the photo and she moved to the side of the bed. She held Peggy's delicate hand, now gone limp and cold. Susan laid her head on Peggy's shoulder and put her arm over her chest, feeling the faint beat of Peggy's heart and hearing her shallow breathing. And then, it was over. Susan took the photo she was holding, held it close to her heart for a moment and put it back in Peggy's hand. Whatever secret it held should rest with Peggy, Susan thought, not her.

At the funeral, the hospice chaplain handed Susan an envelope and said this was her aunt's personal item and she should have it. Susan put it in her purse, planning to open it later.

After the funeral and internment, Susan wandered the rooms of Peggy's house. As the executrix and Peggy's only surviving kin, it was Susan's job to clear out ninety-six years of Peggy's accumulated memories. It wasn't a large house, but every room overflowed with knick-knacks, photos, and a variety of personal items. Peggy had inherited her mother's silver, china, and crystal, which filled an entire breakfront. There were several large oil portraits of long dead and unknown relatives. A bureau in the dining room contained a host of neatly ironed and folded table linens. There was a small Duncan Phyfe secretary in the parlor where Susan found the financial records she needed to close accounts and distribute her aunt's estate.

During the second week of sorting through the house, Susan was emptying Peggy's clothes from her dresser drawers. In the back of the lingerie drawer, she found a stack of six leather books, each tied closed with a blue satin ribbon. Each book had a label with a span of years. The top book label read 1908 to 1918. Susan pulled up the shades on the windows for more light, sat down on the bed and opened the first book. It was a diary, neatly written in Peggy's well-practiced, elegant cursive. Every entry was dated, and the first page of the first book read May 24, 1908, Peggy's tenth birthday. The last entry in the last book was May 2, 1994, three weeks before she died. As Susan skimmed each diary it was obvious there were not daily entries, and often long stretches of time between entries, in one case five years and another time seven years. Many of the entries were short, one sentence or two. For these diaries to span eighty-six years was incredible. How fascinating, Susan thought, to have this record of her long life. As Susan began to read the first diary, the memory of the photo in Peggy's hand flashed through her mind. She flipped through the pages until she came to July 17, 1916 and there it was; the reference to the photograph. It read:

Had a great day on the boardwalk today with Helen and Dottie. We swam in the morning, ate lunch at that cute new sandwich shop, and ran into James as we were heading for home. A strolling photographer was taking pictures and selling them for $.50. James insisted we get one and he paid the man to make four copies, one for each of us. What fun. I will cherish this photo forever.

The entry for July 27, 1916 read:

The photo arrived today. We look wonderful. I think I'll get a nice frame for this and put it on the dresser in my bedroom. I really like James and he seems to like me too. Maybe he'll ask me for a date soon. My heart flutters when I see him. I hope he feels the same.

Susan flipped through the next few entries and stopped when her eyes fell on the word "pregnant." It was dated December 27, 1916.

I'm three months pregnant with James' baby. What am I going to do? I can't tell my mother and father or even my sister. I went to a doctor in Georgetown. I'll have to tell James, I hope he will want to marry me because if he doesn't I might have to kill myself.

Who was this James? Did he even have a last name? Susan's mind flooded with questions about this man and his relationship to her aunt Peggy. Backtracking and reading every word from July 1916 she learned that James and Peggy had started dating in August 1916 and progressed rapidly from handholding to passionate sex; a whirlwind affair fueled by the fresh sea air, the summer breezes, long walks on the beach, and the hormones of youth. Peggy was hoping for a proposal of marriage at either Thanksgiving or Christmas, but James didn't oblige. In fact, there was even a hint that James had been flirting with Helen.

Filled with curiosity, Susan read hungrily until the baby was born. James, learning of Peggy's pregnancy had urged her to "get rid of it," and gave her the name of a doctor in Philadelphia who could "take care of it." Peggy was devastated. She refused. James broke off with her and started dating Helen. Peggy left for New York with the excuse of going to study art. Her parents never knew about the baby. He was born in New York City and, according to the diary, given up for adoption. The entry for July 3, 1917 read:

Today I signed the papers to give up my son for adoption. It is the worst day of my life, but I know it is the right thing to do. I delivered him at the New York Foundling Hospital on June 17 and they have found a wonderful family for him. They live in Irvington, NY and the father is a successful attorney. It will be a good home for him. I made a copy of the photo of James and me on the boardwalk last year and I tucked it in his blanket when I gave him to the nurse.

Startled, Susan put her hand over her mouth. June 17 was her father's birthday. Irvington was his hometown. His father was an attorney. Wait, this can't be possible, she thought as tears slid down her cheeks. Could Peggy's baby be her father? Did Peggy know? Was that why Peggy was so attached to her, why she doted on her from the time she was born? Was she really Susan's grandmother? Susan needed answers, but with no living relatives to ask she didn't know where to start to find them.

Then she remembered her DNA test. If her father, William, really was Peggy's son, then a DNA test might prove a genetic link through her DNA. There must be some of Peggy's DNA here somewhere. Scanning the room, her eyes saw a hairbrush on the vanity. Susan carefully pulled out as much hair as possible, put it in an envelope, and slipped it into her purse. As she was about to close her purse, she noticed the envelope the hospice chaplain had given her. She opened the envelope to find the photograph of the three close friends and James taken in happier times. Susan stared at the photo a long time trying to see if there were any resemblance in her family to this James. Could James be her grandfather? Perhaps the eyes, but the photo was black and white so she couldn't determine their color although the shape reminded her of own eyes. The cleft in his chin was the same as her son's. She reluctantly tucked the photo back into her purse as the mantle clock struck four p.m. and Susan knew she must get back to the work of cleaning out the house.

Later that evening, when everything was either ready for the thrift shop or the furniture dealer, Susan went to the bedroom to retrieve the diaries. She picked up the stack and put them in her tote bag along with Peggy's financial records. I'll read these diaries tomorrow, she thought, maybe they'll have some additional information. Then, as she closed the front door and locked it, Susan whispered, "Good night, Aunt Peggy. I hope you are resting in peace. If I find out you are my grandma, I'll wish I had known it before you died so I could have called you Nana. Love you with all my heart." Susan blew a kiss to the stars, got into her van and drove off, smiling at the coming adventure of unraveling the mystery of Peggy's baby and her own heritage.

Soaring

by Russell Reece

It was drizzling when Father drove me to the station in Harrington. We sat in the car waiting for the train, water dripping onto my cape, me staring at the grayness, at nothing really. I had been that way for over a week now.

Father took my hand. "You've got to buck up, Bess," he said. "The memorial service this evening will be difficult. Rose and Charles's mother will need your strength."

I leaned against his shoulder. "How can I be strong for others? I've yet to find it in myself." The crinkling of his canvas slicker against my cheek diminished any comfort I might have had. "It's as though something has been let out of me."

He pulled me tight against him. "Charles was a fine young man."

The rails clicked beneath the car as the train wound through the damp woods and fields of lower Delaware. The rain had finally stopped and sunlight struggled through a partially overcast sky. I looked around the train-car at groups of picnickers heading for an Indian summer getaway at the beach. I envied their gay clothing and joyful mood. I pulled Rose's letter from my bag. The newspaper clipping slipped from the envelope and I read it for the hundredth time.

September 20, 1918 - Lieutenant Charles W. Bean, II, U.S. Army, killed in France in June 1918 during the battle of Belleau Wood when his observation aircraft was shot down by German machinegun fire. Lieutenant Bean, a resident of Rehoboth Beach, Delaware, was among 1,800 fellow Americans who gave their lives at Belleau Wood in the cause of freedom.

My hands still trembled when I read the words, but the shock and sadness I had initially felt had been replaced with anger. I was angry Beanie had been missing for months before they discovered the wreckage and confirmed he was dead. I was angry our brave doughboys who had given their lives were put to rest in faraway places no one has ever heard of. I was angry at President Wilson and all the government men who took our country into this horrible war for a cause that was not our own.

I slumped against the wooden back of my seat and looked out the window, anxious about seeing Rose again, wondering if Ethel would be there. Rose was Beanie's sister. She and I were born in 1900 three days apart. Our family's summer place was on the same street as their residence in Rehoboth and over the years we had grown close.

Ethel is Rose's cousin, a year older than us. She lives in Philadelphia and visits each summer for several weeks. The three of us are inseparable when Ethel's around.

Beanie was two years older than Ethel. We all looked up to him as a big brother. He took care of us when we were growing up and delighted in having three willing participants for his boyhood escapades. He had such a great imagination. One year he "found" a treasure map "stained in blood." We became his band of pirates and followed him around the fields and up and down the dune, our stick-swords at the ready and a shovel at hand. I can't imagine the number of holes we dug trying to find the "rusty chest of gold and jewels" he convinced us would be there.

I laughed out loud at the thought, then quickly covered my mouth with my hand and glanced around the train-car to make sure no one had heard.

Everyone in town liked Beanie. He was outgoing and good natured, always willing to help. As he grew older he became known for his skills at fixing things, probably due to his curiosity about technology. Mrs. Bean said he almost wore out the switch watching the light go on and off when they first installed the electrics in '09. He was fascinated by telephones and by every new automobile that showed up in town. But most of all he was enthralled with flying machines. He had seen one in 1910 when he was thirteen. When he learned the first flight had taken place on a beach in North Carolina, it was all he could talk about. It was as if his living at the beach made him part of it somehow.

Mr. Bean said it was just a circus stunt, that nothing would ever come of airplanes and flying, but Beanie didn't care, said he would be a flier someday. He was so earnest. Ethel, Rose and I made fun of him, called him bird-boy. One day he snatched the canvas spread we used on the sand, held it aloft, his arms wide apart and flew down the beach. We chased after, to the delight of Mrs. Bean. Beanie darted this way and that until we all plopped in the sand in exhaustion. He kept soaring, up and down the dune, the canvas flapping behind like a pennant in the wind.

Rose met me at the train in Rehoboth. On the ride down, I had rehearsed what I would say but when I saw her no words would come. We embraced, held each other, and cried as passengers and trainmen walked by. Mother would have said it was a poor display for two young ladies who knew better, but I didn't care. It was what I needed, and the way Rose held me, perhaps what we both needed. Afterward, she took my bag and we walked to the buggy. I grasped her arm, not wanting to lose touch lest I succumb again to the sadness I'd felt on the ride down. The mare turned and looked at us as we approached.

"I thought you were getting a car," I said.

"I told you we would be one of the last, but I think it is close," Rose said. "Father had talked about it every day, until the news."

We climbed aboard. Rose took the reins, clicked her tongue and called out to Dolly. She turned the horse toward home. The lurch of the rig, the cantor and cadence of hoof beats on the sand was surprisingly comforting to me. My father had gotten an automobile two years earlier and sold our horse and buggy. "This is nice," I said. "Sometimes the world goes by too quickly in a car."

"How are your mother and father?" I asked.

"When we first received the letter Mother was hysterical. It was frightening, but she quickly recovered and has steeled herself almost beyond understanding. Father remains distraught. He rarely sleeps; stays at the bank long after it closes. Mother sent me to pick him up yesterday and I found him sitting in his office with the lights out."

My thought returned to Beanie and a wave of sadness washed through me again.

"I am hopeful, after tonight things will improve," Rose said. Our gazes met for a moment. I wondered if my eyes were as tired and sad.

The road led through the park along the newly completed Lewes canal. It was nice to see the landscaping had taken hold so well. "Have you heard from Ethel?" I asked.

"We exchanged letters. I don't expect her at the service. She's so tied up in the fight for the vote. After the National Women's Party bill was defeated last year it's all she thinks of."

"I wonder if this movement is not a lot to do about nothing," I said. "Would the women's vote have kept us from this war?"

"Perhaps it would," Rose said.

I pondered that possibility.

As we approached our lane the familiar roar of the surf sounded over the hoof beats. The air was tinged with the wonderful scent of salt and sea-brine and for just a moment my mind filled with pleasant thoughts of summer days, of sand on my bare feet and of happy forays over the dune. But I was quickly reminded of the sad occasion and chastised myself for being frivolous.

We turned onto our lane with the row of fine houses on the left and the dune bordering on the right. Many of the houses were shuttered for the season including ours which I watched closely as we passed by.

Mr. Lingo's ice wagon was coming up the road. His horse raised and shook its head as if offering a greeting to Dolly. Mr. Lingo held up on the reins and tipped his hat. Rose held up.

"Miss Rose, Miss Bess," he said.

"Hello, Mr. Lingo," I said.

"Such a sad thing." He shook his head, grimaced. "Young Mr. Charles. None better."

"Thank you, Mr. Lingo," Rose said. "You are very kind." She smiled, nodded and then slapped the reins. Dolly moved on. "Everyone means well," she said. "They all loved Beanie, but their condolences are a constant reminder. Perhaps after tonight people will let the healing begin."

Rose's house was the last on the lane. Beyond was an unkempt field with clumps of cutgrass, beach plum, scrub pine and cedar extending north as far as one could see. For just a moment I imagined the four of us out in the field on one of our childhood adventures.

Rose pulled the buggy into the circular drive and stopped in front of the entrance stairs. The house was the largest on the block, of Victorian design with fancywork trimming the wide, wraparound porch. The house had been freshly painted white, the shutters a pale blue. A well-kept stable filled part of the back yard. Mr. Bean's status as a successful banker was evident.

"Shouldn't we put up Dolly?" I asked.

"Mother plans to fetch Father from the bank," Rose said. Just then Mrs. Bean pushed open the front door.

"Bess," she said. She had on a long, dark dress extending to just above her shoes. The bodice hung loose, as if she had lost weight. My gaze stopped at her left arm where she wore a dark band embroidered with a gold star.

She came down the stairs and reached for me. "I'm so happy you were able to come," she said.

"Oh Mrs. Bean, I'm so sorry about Beanie," I said. She hugged me. "I miss him so already." Her hand stroked my back.

After a moment she held me out. The sunlight glinted on the gold embroidery of the star. Her mouth trembled slightly as she pushed a stray hair from my forehead. "It's hard on us all," she said. She smiled and took my arm. "Come, let's get you settled."

Rose and I went up to her room. I took off my cape and was checking myself at her vanity mirror when I saw the photograph mounted in a gold frame. I picked it up. "I'd forgotten about this," I said. I sat next to her on the bed and studied the image taken in the summer of 1916. "It's the day we bobbed our hair. Beanie had found those funny sunshades and we were all feeling so wicked. I remember it all. Look at Ethel, waving, and you so tall and proud with your white parasol." I looked at Beanie and took a deep breath. Rose put her hand on my arm. "Beanie looks so serious."

"That was the summer everyone was arguing about the war. He was so firm, so idealistic. I think he would have forgone engineering school and volunteered with the Brits if Father hadn't talked sense into him."

"I remember. We teased him about being a sourpuss. He didn't take well to it. He called us silly little girls, and not in jest." I suddenly felt guilty at the remembering.

"I guess we were," Rose said.

The day had cleared and the sky was filled with blustery clouds. Mrs. Bean went off to the bank and Rose and I walked across the street and up the path through the dune. The beach was wide here, waves a few feet high, the ocean fairly calm. A group of seagulls stood in a cluster to our left. They watched as we approached.

"I haven't asked about your schooling," Rose said. "How is it going?"

"I'll finish the Normal School in December," I said. "After that I can take the Delaware teacher's exam. Then I don't know. A position will have to open."

"I'm sure one will."

"I hope so. I'm anxious to work with the children." We walked south in the moist sand along the edge of the shoreline. "And you, Rose, have you chosen a direction?"

"Father believes there's a place for me in town. He continues to inquire with the shopkeepers and remains hopeful, but I think nothing will come until the next summer season. Until then I'm helping Mother with the house."

"And what of that boy, Billy McMaster? Is he still calling on you?"

Rose smiled and bit her tongue.

"Oh he is, isn't he?"

She stopped walking and turned toward me. Waves washed ashore behind her. "He comes from time to time."

"You're blushing."

"No I'm not."

"You are." I took her hands. "You must tell me everything." And then her smile faded and her eyes welled with tears. Her hands tightened on mine.

"Oh, Bess. We talk about our future, our plans, and the joys of our lives with Beanie's remains lying in some field in France. Are we being silly again?"

A wave of sorrow fell back over me. I hugged her. "Sometimes it's so hard to know," I said.

When we got back to the house Mr. Bean was walking from the stable. He greeted me; smiling and genuine as always, but his normally energetic demeanor had changed. He almost seemed brittle, as if his spirit had stolen away and left the shell of his body behind. He took my hand. "Thank you for coming, Bess."

I struggled for words again. He nodded. "I know," he said. He patted my hand.

"Father wanted to come but was unable to leave."

"He wrote a letter. It meant a great deal to me."

The grove at the camp-meeting chapel was filled with automobiles and a handful of buggies. A place in front had been kept for the Beans and as we drove up, a soldier in uniform took the horse and held it still while Mrs. Bean was helped down by another. A third, elderly soldier stood at attention near the chapel door holding a staff with an American flag. Most of the city's residents were present and many paid their respects to the family. Rose and I moved through the crowd visiting with friends. We were talking to Billy McMasters and his mother when a bell sounded. We turned to see the reverend at the door. "Friends," he said, beckoning everyone inside. "We are about to start."

The two soldiers offered their arms to Mrs. Bean and to Rose and escorted them in with Mr. Bean and me trailing behind. We sat down in the front row. I closed my eyes and over the murmur of the crowd filing into the chapel, said a quick prayer for Beanie.

The reverend began the service by leading the congregation in the singing of "Amazing Grace." He then opened the podium for any wishing to testify. Several men came forward and spoke kind words about Beanie which brought both tears and laughter. It was gratifying to see how his good nature and character had made such a mark on the community. Afterwards, the reverend offered a touching prayer for fallen servicemen, where at one point Mr. Bean cried out, his effort to stifle his emotion apparently failing and magnifying it instead. Mrs. Bean, her right hand on her husband's shoulder, a hanky in her left, consoled him through the heartrending moment.

During the sermon the reverend spoke of Jesus raising Lazarus from the dead and how our spirits never die but remain and abide with the Holy Father. Beanie would be with us forever, in our hearts and our memories. And then we sang "In the Sweet By and By" which filled the chapel with a peaceful resonance. In the end, the solemn place, the joining of the community and the reverend's confident, plainspoken words left me comforted and reassured. I also saw a change in Mr. Bean, as if there had been some kind of release in him. After the service, I knew he would be okay.

Rose and I got ready for bed shortly after returning home. Her room was on the corner of the house with two large windows, one facing the ocean. We talked for a while and then sat and watched the moon and the stars, each lost in our own reverie. It seemed a fitting end to the day. As I got into bed the photo caught my eye again. We'll never be the same, I thought, but how lucky we were to have had each other and to have grown up in this special place. I switched off the lamp and was asleep in moments.

When I woke, the sun was bright. Rose was standing at the window looking down into the side-yard. I stretched and yawned.

"I'm worried about Mother," she said. "It's not even seven and she's washed and hung the laundry."

I got up and looked. The clothesline was filled with linens billowing in the breeze. "She must have hung them in the dark," I said. "They seem already dry."

We dressed and made the bed. Downstairs the table was set. Mr. Bean had left for the bank and as we entered the dining room Mrs. Bean placed a covered platter of eggs and bacon on the table. "Good morning," Rose said.

Mrs. Bean barely smiled as she poured us juice from a glass pitcher. She went back to the kitchen without saying a word. Rose looked at me with a perplexed expression. "Will you join us, Mother?" she asked.

"I've too much to do," she said from behind the door.

"Let us finish breakfast and we'll help you," Rose said.

The screen door slapped shut. Rose got up from the table and looked out the window. She gasped. "Mother!"

Mrs. Bean sat on the stairs with her laundry basket in her lap. She was slumped against the porch-post, a hand covering her face, her body convulsed in tears. Rose sat down beside and took her in her arms.

"I thought if I could just get through the service…" Tears streamed down. In a whisper she said, "I miss him so."

"Oh, Mrs. Bean," I said. "Beanie would be so sad to see you like this. He would only want the best for you, for us all."

Mrs. Bean straightened up and wiped her nose. "When he last came home, after his flight training, he was so handsome in his uniform." She looked at Rose.

"He was," Rose said.

"His father and I were so proud of him," Mrs. Bean said. She smiled. "He said he wanted to take me up. Imagine that, me in an airplane." She laughed. "He said I would love it. He said he would teach me to fly." She looked at us, her smile withering. "He was such a dear." She covered her face and wept.

A wild look came over Rose. She darted up, pulled several table linens off the line and tossed all but one onto the porch stairs. I thought she must have gone crazy.

"Beanie has already taught us to fly, Mother," she said. She spread the tablecloth between outstretched arms.

Mrs. Bean hesitated, but then stood, grabbed a cloth of her own and spread her wings. I did as well. And then we flew across the road, over the dune and out onto the beach. Mrs. Bean stopped, but waved her linen and cheered us on. I know Beanie was watching us and laughing as Rose and I flew and flew.

The Hill Girls

by Gail Braune Comorat

The story changed every time it was told. The man in the photo was someone different depending on which sister was holding the frame. Once the photograph came down from the wall, the three sisters began talking at once—all reminiscing about that summer of 1916, the last year their father was alive, the year the middle sister married and she and her husband took over their father's small family guesthouse in the heart of Rehoboth.

Their arguments about the man's identity changed weekly.

Of course, the man was Lily's fiancé. Eliza was sure of that. It was definitely Eddie.

No, the man was obviously Lucky Lindy, Mattie said. He'd landed his plane in a nearby cornfield. They'd all swooned when they met him! That thick hair! So handsome.

Goodness, Lily said. I'd know my own man, wouldn't I? That is not Eddie.

My daughter, Jane, and I met the sisters the summer before Jane headed off to college. She and I stayed for a month in one of their guest rooms, and they all took an instant liking to my girl. Something about Jane reminded them of the baby sister they'd lost more than sixty years earlier.

She's a dead-ringer for Sarah, Lily said. It's the wide eyes. So blue. Sarah was the only one of us who got the blue eyes. Just like Daddy's.

More the mouth, I believe, Mattie said as she touched Jane's lips and nodded. Yes, this girl has my same cupid's bow. Neither of you has it, but Sarah surely did. And so does Jane.

Eliza insisted that Jane had their sister's neck. Like a swan, she said. Exactly like Sarah's neck, so long and elegant.

Jane asked if they had a picture of Sarah, and they all shook their heads.

Oh, if only we did, Eliza said.

But seeing Jane is almost like having Sarah back, said Lily.

Someone take a picture, Mattie said. Stand here beside me, Jane!

I was the photographer that day, seeing the four of them through my lens, thinking that my daughter looked as if she were posing with distant ancestors. They were right—Jane had Mattie's lovely mouth, beautiful wide eyes, a graceful neck.

The ladies served high tea in the dining room every Sunday. They sat with us that very first Sunday, the three of them on the velvet banquette, backs to the wall, eyes on the room. They took turns, rising to greet guests, to check that the sandwiches and pastries on the mahogany sideboard didn't need replenishing. Young waiters passed trays of food, poured tea. Jane and I weren't used to such fancy service. The fragile teacups, the silver gleaming on pressed linen tablecloths. I felt awkward and overly large for the dainty chair I sat in, maybe a bit like Alice in Wonderland when she ate the cookie and grew too large for the room. I had my father's bones, his wide shoulders, his generous hands and feet, as he called them. I was thankful Jane had not inherited any of that. She was as small as the three Hill Girls. Her wavy bobbed hair made her look even more like one of them.

Jane noticed the photograph on the wall right away. Is that the three of you? she asked, pointing to a spot behind Lily, where dozens of faded photos in dark, carved frames hung on the flocked wallpaper. People strolling on the boardwalk or posing on the beach, all black and white shots. Sepia, Jane said later when I talked about the photos. Even then, she always knew the right word. She was heading to the university to study writing, thinking maybe she'd teach high school one day. Her plans were still flexible; the world was hers that summer.

I remember how Eliza twisted around to see which picture Jane indicated, and how Eliza's eyebrows shot up and her mouth widened as if she'd never before noticed the photo hanging there. Mattie was already reaching for it. She was the youngest of the sisters, always the quickest to react.

Look how young we were, Eliza said when Mattie handed her the picture. Look at you, Mattie, being cheeky as always. And, Lily! I think you look quite smug for some reason. Who is that man beside you? Where are my glasses?

Her glasses were always hanging around her neck, dangling from a fob-like pearl chain. I noticed that she was also wearing small pearl earrings and a pearl ring on her right hand, while Mattie wore no jewelry at all, and Lily wore a single gold band on her left hand.

Eliza was the eldest, the most proper of the three. I liked the way Mattie and Lily treated her, how they both always seemed to let her have the last word when they told their stories.

In the photo, she's leaning in beside Mattie, who is in the center. I remember thinking that Eliza was the most beautiful of the three, but really, they were all lovely in their summer dresses. Jane called the fabric *lawn*.

It's Eddie, you ninny. Mattie took back the photo and said: That's why she's so smug, Eliza. She knew she would be the only one of us to marry.

She knew no such thing. I too had a beau that summer, Eliza said. That gentleman from Philadelphia. Don't you remember?

I think I wore my hair with a henna rinse that year, Lily said. See? It's lighter than yours, Eliza, and we always had the same color, but that year I was trying something new.

Well, I had the curls, Mattie said. Natural curls. She wound a finger through her short white bangs, then used both hands to fluff the short sides.

Mattie was the one looking smug that day, I thought. They must have all been in their late seventies and early eighties the year we stayed there because once, toward the end of our vacation, Mattie let it slip that she turned nineteen that September of 1916. She said she was jealous that Lily, only thirteen months her senior, was about to be married in October.

I wasn't much older than you, but back then we married young, she said to Jane as we studied the photograph. Mattie held onto Jane's arm with both hands. She was the touchy-feely one, always hugging and kissing everyone right on the lips before you had a chance to turn your cheek. No wonder

Eliza called her cheeky. I liked Eliza. She had dignity and poise. I liked Lily too. So did Jane. We hated that she'd been such a young widow. Married less than two years.

But Mattie was Jane's favorite; she called her spunky, loved her quick wit. Jane and I were both surprised that Mattie had never married. She certainly loved men—she talked about them all the time, and even flirted with the male guests at Sunday tea, no matter their age. Jane would say, Uh oh. Mattie's on the prowl again!

The sisters called themselves The Hill Girls. Even though Lily had married and taken her husband's name, she still called herself a Hill Girl. We Hill Girls love our little beach town, she said. We Hill Girls serve a proper tea, Eliza said. We Hill Girls have had the best adventures, Mattie said. In her letters from school, Jane always wrote that she couldn't wait to see The Hill Girls again; I loved seeing The Hill Girls in capital letters, as if they were the title of a book or movie.

The man in the photo was certainly a mystery. Sometimes, when The Hill Girls talked about him, he was identified as F. Scott Fitzgerald. The sisters told us how he and Zelda rented a house in Wilmington one year, but the famous couple loved to come to Rehoboth Beach for long weekends.

Anonymously, of course! Eliza said. He wore dark glasses and a straw hat so that no one would recognize him! When she told the story, she clutched her hands together to her chest, and her voice got breathy, making her sound like a girl in her twenties.

They stayed in your room, Lily said to us. The very same room!

When the man in the photo was identified as Fitzgerald, Mattie would lean in and elaborate that he invited them up to Wilmington for a party one weekend. An estate, it was, she whispered. A proper estate with landscaped grounds and a long gravel driveway. Zelda danced on tabletops! Scotty drank champagne from her shoes!

The house had twenty-five bedrooms and was perched on a hill overlooking the river, Lily said. I think we went in autumn. Was it that year? Had I married Eddie then? She always seemed the fuzziest about the stories. Always asked her sisters to corroborate her memories. Sometimes she was the one to begin the story, but she often drifted off, unsure of what had taken place in the tale she was telling.

There was a peacock! Walking across their lawn, Mattie said. Each time she told us that, she clapped her hands as if a distant memory had suddenly become clear.

Was there? Lily always asked.

Once, the man in the picture was a redhead, an heir to the Wanamaker fortune. Mattie had a fondness for redhead-ed men, and she'd befriended him on the boardwalk when she'd offered him some popcorn. Once, he was one of the Wilmington du Ponts, and Eliza had almost married him. Except, Mattie remembered reading in the gossip magazines that he was already secretly engaged to a horse-faced woman he'd met at boarding school.

Eliza was always our beauty, said Lily.

Pish-posh, Eliza said.

Later, Jane loved rehashing their stories in her letters from school. Who was the mystery man? she asked. Of course, we knew by then that he couldn't have been either Charles Lindbergh or F. Scott Fitzgerald. Jane had looked them up in the university's library, and learned that Lindbergh hadn't flown his first Jenny until 1923, and Fitzgerald didn't rent the Wilmington mansion until 1927. F. Scott would have been twenty in that 1916 photograph, so perhaps he'd been there years before he became famous. But Lucky Lindy would have been about fourteen years old in 1916! We speculated that perhaps the sisters really did meet them later in life, but got confused with the time. They certainly seemed to recall some specific details.

Jane wondered if the man's name might be noted on the back of the photo. Even though the date and place had been inked on the front of the picture, maybe one of The Hill Girls had written their names and his on the reverse side. Jane said next summer she was going to ask the sisters to pry off the back of the frame to check. She wanted the puzzle solved.

The day that Jane and I packed our bags to head home, Mattie hugged us and made us promise we'd return the very next summer. So we booked the same room for the following July. Another summer month with The Hill Girls. They all kissed us goodbye that day. I remember Lily waving, calling out to us as we drove away: Goodbye, Sarah! Goodbye! Jane and I had laughed about how she'd mistaken Jane for her long-dead sister.

Only Eliza was still living the last time I stayed at the guest-house in 1994. She was selling it, moving into a new residence for seniors. She was turning one hundred that year, and more than a little sad that her sisters weren't there to celebrate with her. Mattie had died only two years earlier. Lily, almost a dozen years before that.

My Jane had died the spring of her freshman year. A fever, some aches. Minor complaints over the phone, and I had said the semester was almost over, that she'd feel better once she got home. All she needed was a little rest and some of my chicken soup.

Meningitis. The dorm director said, If only she'd gone to the infirmary.

I didn't want to tell the sisters over the phone, so I went back to the beach by myself, told them about Jane in person. They surrounded me in the foyer, holding me and weeping with me. Mattie hurried off to her room and brought back the photo I'd taken of Jane and The Hill Girls that first day. One of them had written wobbly letters at the bottom: Jane and Us 1976.

Our little Jane, said Eliza.

Gone. Like Sarah, Lily said.

Poor Sarah. She fell asleep and never woke up, Mattie said. The youngest Hill Girl.

I was glad I returned in 1977. High tea was a good memory, that month of Sundays when I had sat with Jane and The Hill Girls. I remembered the way Jane had pointed to the photo the first time, and asked: Is that the three of you? It became a weekly ritual after that, Jane pointing to the photo and saying something like, Look how happy you all are in that picture! Or, I wonder who is the handsome man in that photo? Jane and I had loved how the women told the story differently every time, the way the anonymous man was someone famous or important in their lives.

From that summer on, I was the one who had to ask about the picture. I was the one who listened to the stories. There was no Jane to laugh with afterwards.

It wasn't until Eliza's last summer in her guesthouse that I thought to ask if she'd ever looked on the back of the photograph to see if anything was written there. We were sharing high tea, and on that day we'd been speaking about her sisters and Jane. I told her how much my girl had loved her summer with them, how she wrote about them in every letter, calling them The Hill Girls. How she'd planned to ask them if we could pry away the frame's back to look for the man's name.

Pry off the back? Well, Jane was certainly smarter than the rest of us, Eliza said. She nodded and motioned for me to use my butter knife to do just that.

Jane's hunch had been a good one. On the back of the photograph, in spidery letters, someone had written: Eliza, Mattie, Lily and an illegible capital letter that was blurred as if a single tear had fallen on it. Was it an E? An F? It even could have been an L.

Jane would have loved that the letter was indecipherable, how it added even more mystery to that old photograph.

She and I would have talked about it for years to come.

Last Letter

Eve of the Battle of Saint-Mihiel, Second Battle of the Somme Campaign

by James Keegan

September 11, 1918

My dearest Rose,

Before all else, I want you to know that your letter dated July 30th arrived yesterday (pretty fast, considering) and lifted my heart greatly, most especially the photograph you enclosed from our Rehoboth excursion summer before last. I'd not seen that picture before but I remember Uncle Mike getting us to pose and remember well the day and the great time we all had. You and Win and Lizzie all look ready for the moving pictures with your parasols and Wilson goggles. "Three blind mice, see how they run . . ." Ha, ha, ha!

A funny thing, Rose, is that I thought when I first saw the photograph how you look like my sisters in it. I'd never thought that before and then a fellow in my outfit who was looking over my shoulder at the time asked me if those were my sisters in the picture. How about that? I told him two were but the other was my fiancée—and when he asked me which I made him guess, and I didn't get to ask him what decided him, but he picked you out right away. It's silly, I know, but it made me happy when he did. It surprised me too since I'm rather leaning away from you and toward the girls. Or maybe he just pointed to the prettiest, eh? I'd say that was it. Of course, I forget too that we were only starting our "lean" toward each other that summer, with no notion we would be where we are now. Have I told you enough that you've made me the happiest fellow I know?

Thank you too for sending the clipping with Andrew's poem. He must have popped a few vest buttons when he saw his work in print! He has a lovely way with words, that brother of yours—tell him I said those Loyola Jesuits are learnin' him good. I miss the lectures and seminars myself and look forward to finishing up my studies there when I get back. You know, of course, that I am more for the sciences than the arts, so I appreciate all you Connellys striving to give me some introduction to the fine and the philosophical. I won't fib to you, Rose. I don't think I fully understand what Andrew is trying to say in the poem. Is it about the war? It seems it might be, though I'm not sure I can say why. When he talks about the "bright maple leaves filling the drain" and the two small boys lying face down on the bank with their "hands dangling in the water," it filled me with a sorrow. You didn't explain it at all in your letter, which, I think I should warn you, can only mean you think me a good deal cleverer than I am. Though I do know that I could "love with a love that was more than a love in our kingdom by the sea." See that, I remember. That was another wonderful time from that summer seaside trip.

Tomorrow we will be part of the first completely American drive. I cannot express to you how it makes me feel to know I will be there to do my share in the cause, such joy and pride. I know you are all fretting over me and praying for me, but I want to tell you that you need not be afraid. You will see by my steady penmanship that I have no terror of what might befall me. That you are there waiting, my dear one, makes me believe I will come through and come home.

Whatever happens, I will never regret my decision to be part of our force here. I believe our cause is clean and just. We could not sit idly by across the ocean when our presence could make the difference and bring this long conflict to its proper end. I know that has been hard for you to accept at times, my Rose, but I can tell you that I believe my having been here will only make our future together better, more meaningful, our life more sweet. I have had some small chance as we have moved up toward the line to watch medics and doctors at work here, and their calm under pressure and their ability to do so much good in hard circumstances has confirmed for me that I am on the right path for me. For us.

Well, my dearest one, the lantern has burned down so I must close this letter. Keep the home fires burning for me. Please look after mother so she will not worry over much and tell all at home how much I miss and love them, but, of course, none more than you, popinjay. Continue to scout the neighborhood for where we'll set up house once we are wed. You've got better sense for all that than I do. I carry your locket in my breast pocket, next to my heart, where I carry you.

May God bless and keep you, dearest love.
David

5. MAN AND WOMAN IN BATHING SUITS

Photo Courtesy of Rehoboth Beach Historical Society and Museum

Rehoboth Honeymoon

by Kit Zak

White tongue of blue-gray waves
I watch you lick sand

in teasing repetition,
captivated by your insistent roar,

recalling dawn's golden ball
rising from unknown depths,

and drawn by your hypnotic rhythms
swell—crest—break—retreat

I succumb and plunge my body
face-first into foam, uniting with billowing brine

skin chilled, heart pounding
I am whole—I am free.

6. COTTAGES

Photo Courtesy of Rehoboth Beach Historical Society and Museum

A Wish and a Prayer

by Terri Clifton

Rebecca slid sideways on the wooden trestle bench, making room for her mother to join her at the table. There were tired creases around her mother's kind and faded hazel eyes, and Rebecca tried to remember if they'd always been there. She smiled and kept slicing peaches.

Her mother picked up a whole one from the basket and began to peel it. The knife slid effortlessly beneath the fuzzy skin. "These peaches are a bit sour. A little more sugar than I'd usually use, I think. We don't need any sour faces to go with it. That would ruin the photograph."

Everyone in the camp was excited for tomorrow. A real photographer from Dover, her Papa said, but she'd heard from Cleota Davis it was Wilmington, and that he was a newspaperman, too, coming to document the Rehoboth ministry and promote the ideals of the meeting camp. There was even to be a picnic afterward, a last celebration before they all left for the year.

It had been a hard, cold winter. Even the old people said it was more snow than they'd ever seen. The lakes and rivers froze. Animals perished, and people got sick. Rebecca had been more than ready to spend a few weeks at the seaside, even if it meant that everyone else there was praying and preaching. She'd use her prayers for her momma, who seemed to grow thinner and paler every day.

When the cobbler was readied and the Dutch oven nestled into the coals, Rebecca sat on the porch to mend the hem of the only good skirt she'd packed. She could hear the waves reaching the shore in the darkness beyond her lantern light.

In a few more days, they'd be home. She wasn't looking forward to being back on the farm, and wondered if her mother could withstand another deep-cold, dark season. She'd taken on more of the work, to ease the burden, but it wasn't enough. Her father never seemed to notice the weakening, or the exhaustion, still expecting all the chores to be done and supper placed before him, to say grace over. Rebecca would listen to him read from the Bible, but she never saw anything like love in his eyes.

Summer was nearly over. It hadn't rained at all for almost a month and every day had been picture perfect. She'd seen dolphins leaping, and a moon that came up so big and pink that Reverend James started singing a hymn. Rebecca wasn't sure if he did it because he was feeling faithful, or fearful. All she knew was that it was wondrous and made her heart beat faster just to watch it climb into the sky. She had a box of seashells tucked into her suitcase, to help her remember. Her sewing complete, she brushed her hair and went to sleep.

The next morning was as bright and perfect as the day before, but it started off cooler, and the sun's rays felt gentler. She tipped her face toward it, caring nothing for the freckles it was bringing to her complexion, scattered across her nose.

They assembled in front of the Donovans' cottage. There were about forty people and Mr. Graves's horse, Hickory. Chairs were brought out, but most people sat on the ground and the back row stood. The children were warned against squirming and were largely patient with the process. The photographer was indeed from Wilmington and Rebecca watched him set up the camera, a box on legs. It felt strange to hold herself frozen, surrounded by people doing the same. Sand had found its way into her shoes and stockings, and she wiggled her toes in an effort to keep the rest of herself still.

She examined the man standing behind the camera. He paid little attention to the group other than issuing instructions, focused on his gadgetry and his craft. There was nothing extraordinary about him. She had thought he would look more dashing.

He made three photographs. The horse moved for the second and wasn't included in the third. A toddler that had been perched on the animal's back was resettled on the lap of his mother, and the final frame was exposed. Everyone stood and brushed off sand, the women fetching the food while the men gathered to talk. It was only later, after the meal and the prayers, the cobbler and pies eaten, after ease and languor had overtaken the men and the children, and after the women had straightened and cleaned, that Rebecca slipped away. Down to the very edge of the water, her shoes abandoned at the high tide line, she relished the coolness of the water as it touched her toes. She held her skirt just high enough to avoid soaking it, not so high as to lose her modesty.

The ocean was calm. Only the smallest of waves curled against the shore, the surface running like silvered glass all the way to the horizon making it impossible to tell where the sky began. She let her mind drift and daydream, something she almost never did; imagining crossing the wide water, seeing what the rest of the world was like.

When a shadow fell next to her, she started from her reverie and turned. It was the photographer walking closer.

"I didn't mean to startle you, Miss. I wanted you to know I made a photograph of you here just now that I think will be quite nice. You against the wide openness. Lovely."

She didn't know what to say. Her father surely wouldn't approve, and she wasn't at all sure how she felt about it. She just stared at him.

"You seemed so engrossed. I knew if I asked in advance I'd lose what I was trying to capture. I'm sorry if I've offended."

"Oh, no," she said, still unsure, but he looked contrite. He had a kindly face now that he wasn't concentrating. "I was just…imagining." She shocked herself with the ease of her confession to a stranger.

"The sea will do that to you. You know there are people on the other side doing just what you're doing now."

She laughed to think of it. "It's so big. It must be fearful to cross."

"It isn't so bad most of the time."

"You've done it?"

"I have."

"What's it like?" She heard too much in her own voice, and blushed. He pretended not to notice and she thought he might be a gentleman. He didn't laugh at her ignorance.

"Well, it is different from America. Lots of countries close and all. I think Ireland is the prettiest. It's very green. I like Cornwall in England. Have you read about King Arthur and his Knights?"

She shook her head.

He told her about France and England and Spain. She had trouble making pictures in her mind, but loved the sound of his voice, hearing the names of places she didn't dare long to see, amazed that she had thought him ordinary at the start. He couldn't be more than ten years older than she was, and he had been so far. So caught up was she that she lost track of time and realized with a start that the sun was nearly down.

"I must go." She turned to retrieve her shoes. The tide was receding, widening the beach. A seagull called as it passed over.

"Shall I send you a copy of your photograph?"

She was glad he had taken it, but her father would be scandalized that she'd allowed it without his consent. He'd find it vain and unseemly, and that was without knowing she'd spent a long hour with a man she didn't know.

She shook her head and glanced down the beach to the cottages in a row. The first lanterns had been lit. When she looked back he was staring at her with something like sadness. "I can't."

He nodded, and she started to walk away.

"Rebecca."

She hadn't told him her name. She turned back slightly.

"I hope you get to see it."

She knew how unlikely that was, but she smiled because she'd been raised to. As she walked away, she passed the camera, still where it had captured her. She thought of her tiny image held inside, and wondered who would ever see her.

Cottages

by Anne Colwell

The Tuesday that Silas took whiskey again after he'd promised never, I woke to find him on the cold stone of the entryway, propped between the two doors. Beyond the outside door, the morning delivery horses blew and stamped, a boy called the day's headlines, mockingbirds in the azalea scolded. Silas half sat, half lay, asleep above the boater in his lap that he'd sicked up into. I looked at his face, rusty with drink, his stained suit, hands brown with God-knew-what filth, and swallowed my disgust. His stench choked me. I thought of lifting the soiled hat and setting it on his head, but I retreated up the stairs, gathered Josephine, and dressed her.

I put her on my shoulder before opening the door to step over Silas.

"Papa's sleep," she said, and tried to lower her head and look at his pathetic shape stretched there on the stones.

"Indeed," I agreed, lifting her chin with my finger, and we stepped out into the warm day and walked the four blocks to the Reverend Mister Pritchard's house.

His girl showed me in, admired the baby's dress, said she'd return in a moment. I watched her thin back retreat, the white bow of her apron bouncing at her waist, and heard the Reverend's rumbling voice rooms away before he arrived in the parlor, tall and voluble, making the furniture look smaller, booming, "Hello, Delia!" His hand out and a long white napkin at his neck where he had, I supposed, just tucked it in.

"Am I interrupting your meal?" I said. "I can return when…"

"By no means! By no means! Won't you sit? How are you, child?"

He pulled the napkin from his collar, squatted down before Josephine, who reached a wondering hand toward his white hair, unruly always, his wide smiling face.

"We are returning to Philadelphia by the next train," I said. And when the tears came and I could do nothing to stop them, the Reverend took my elbow and moved me to a chair.

"Silas?" he said.

"Damn him all to hell," I spat. And the Reverend went to the back and called the girl who took Josephine's hand and drew her, smiling, toward the kitchen.

Over the course of that long morning, the Reverend Mister Pritchard talked and talked about marriage, the trials and blessings, vows, "a man shall leave his mother, a woman leave her home." I listened to shards of sermons from many weddings, to remembered Bible verses. He talked about his own wife's death, his guilt for all of the moments he failed her. He fought to convince me. "Do nothing rash," he repeated. "Do nothing rash."

I shook my head. "I cannot, I will not go on living like this. I must leave."

"Then go…somewhere else," he said. "Forward, not back. Give God a chance, room to work."

And that is how, somehow—it baffles me even now—somehow, he convinced me and I agreed to take a step far stranger than the logical one of returning to my parents, to the city I knew.

I agreed to a church trip. In two days time, Josephine and I would go to the seaside, to the church cottages where Silas and I had first met, in Cape Henlopen City. I would go alone with Josephine, if need be, or accompanied by Silas, if he could sober up and made to feel enough self-reproach to agree to accompany us.

He could not.

At the start it all seemed a terrible mistake, the whispering ocean, the hot metallic sand, the flat clean light of the shoreline all brought me the girl I'd been seven years before and the boy who I loved, thought I loved, and who existed no more. The boy who had turned into something useless and sad and horrifying. As the horses pulled our caravan toward the low cottages, I looked down at Josephine's face, the fragile pink eyelids, her long dark lashes, and thought, what a terrible world we have brought you into, what a confusing, sad place.

On our arrival, all stood and stretched. The women dusted off their skirts. The men loosed the horses to graze, and some of the boys began playing with a tamer one, one accustomed to the beach, who would come right down on the sand and allow herself to be ridden. She was a beauty, dark brown with a white blaze.

Before we had even unpacked, the Reverend had hired a photographer and arranged us in front of the cottages to have our picture made. In it, I still wear my traveling hat, despite the heat, so does Josephine. She was so small that, standing beside me, she couldn't be seen, and she wouldn't sit in front alone with the other children, cried if she were not touching me. This is the way children are, lightning rods for our fears and sorrows. I looked at the Reverend, and he raised his hand to calm me.

At the last, the photographer instructed that I lift Josephine to the back of the horse. I turned and hesitated—such a tall horse—but a man I hadn't met before, a man with a kind face, seeing my concern, stepped around behind. We both steadied Josephine, our hands touching on either side of her waist. The shock of that hand—I looked away at the last moment from the eye of the camera, keeping the secret.

Almost two years later, after drink took Silas, I married Joseph, the man who held Josephine on the horse that morning. When people who don't know ask if she were named for her father, I've learned to say, "Yes" or sometimes—the mysterious truth—"No. It's coincidence."

7. MAN WITH UMBRELLA

Photo Courtesy of Rehoboth Beach Historical Society and Museum

Sandrilene Looks Back

by Gayla Sullivan

My mother was sure that he had drowned. So were the men of the Rehoboth Beach Fire Company who came to our squat, lime-colored bungalow the afternoon of September 4, 1910 to deliver the news that my father, Edward Carson Bell, had most likely met an untimely death at the end of Horn's Pier the night before. After having gone for an evening swim just before midnight (my mother's part of the story) he had perished in the riptide that had developed in the evening hours (the conclusion of the firefighters and local lifeguards), thereby ending his life in a small, unresolved flourish.

I, on the other hand, was not so sure. My father was bent on tying things up neatly and putting on the finishing touches in every situation—he would sign on the dotted line and write the exact date on legal documents without prompting, he made sure the knives were turned the correct way when my grandmother came to visit for dinner, and he insisted that in all family photographs we posed just so.

It was not like him to just leave us like this.

We had moved to Rehoboth Beach four years earlier when I was six years old. My father's family were Methodists and Eddie (as he was known to his family) had spent summers with his parents at the Summer Camp Meetings beginning in 1873 and lasting till he was almost twelve years old. The promise of summers at the beach whispered to my father as he chopped wood in the icy snare of cold Pennsylvania mornings, and sang to him as March snows melted, turning the hard, packed ribbon of dirt leading up to his family's farm into muddy rivulets. He told me once that when he swam at the beach he liked to think that the water's point-of-origin came from the creek near his home in Monroe County, Pennsylvania, that joined Tobyhanna Creek, which entered the Delaware River, that dumped into the Delaware Bay, and met him in the Atlantic Ocean at Rehoboth Beach.

In other words, his soul was mired in the warm comfort of beach memories, and the beach was mired in his soul. I refused to believe the ocean had taken him. His body had not been found, no decomposed corpse had bobbed up and down in the waves to be discovered by an elderly tourist from Jersey wading into the waters of the Atlantic to cool off. My suspicions became stronger in my ten-year-old mind by two incidents that I have tossed over in my thoughts many times in the middle of the night, those nocturnal moments when most have surrendered to the temporary hiatus of sleep.

The first incident was after the memorial service the Methodists had helped us organize after my father's "death." I had not yet cried, and found the idea of one more of my Pennsylvania relatives saying to me, "You poor dear," unbearable. I had run from the reception in the church basement with its Jell-o rings and warmed-up casseroles to our home two blocks away and kicked off my patent leather shoes, settling into the couch in the front room waiting— wanting—to cry. The afternoon shadows became imperceptibly longer in the quiet of my escape, and I eventually heard my mother walk through the back kitchen door. At first it seemed she was talking to herself, but then it appeared she was speaking to my father. I heard the Irish lilt that came into her voice in unguarded moments.

"Ah, Eddie. Could you not have just admitted that it wasn't working for us? Now your mother and your daughter will always think you're gone, and what good is this life if you can't face down your troubles head on?" There was a silence, and I held my breath. In that moment, perhaps my mother realized I might be on the other side of the door, possibly listening, likely wondering what she was talking about. Did she say "think you're gone?" She called out loudly, "I'm home, darling!" And then, giving herself a few seconds—to recover? to pretend I hadn't heard?—she swept through the kitchen door without a hair out of place (or red, weepy eyes either, I remember thinking) and gave me a brave, wide-eyed smile.

"Now, then. Let's go for a walk on the boardwalk, shall we?" she announced, unpinning the rhinestone brooch from the collar of her black wool mourning dress and stepping out of it, reaching into the linen closet for a lighter dress to walk out and about. "It's a beautiful September afternoon. Your father wouldn't want us moping about. Life is short, my dear!" I couldn't reconcile her cheeriness with the sobbing relatives of a few hours before, and so I went willingly, anxious to leave the suffocation of the afternoon and to feel the ocean breeze near Horn's Pier where my father hadn't really perished (I hoped), to hear the autumn cry of seagulls left behind, and to lose myself in the haze of Rehoboth Beach.

The other event that was inextricably linked with my father's disappearance that September evening was a conversation he and I had had the day before, as we sat on the beach watching a crowd of tourists gather round Howard Pyle, the artist from Wilmington, as he and his family attempted to enjoy a day at the beach. "Poor sod," my father lamented, gazing at the artist's brood of seven children, several of whom were clinging to both him and his wife, "Can't imagine how he ever got any painting done with that lot." He flicked his homemade cigarette into the sand, and suddenly drew closer to me, his voice husky, his eyes piercing. "Listen to me, Sandrilene." Sandrilene was my father's invented name for me; he never called me by my given name, Gloria. Once, when we were sitting on the beach in late August, after the tourists had packed up their beach towels and headed back to town to their dinners and hotels, my father told me that one day he would tell me the adventures of Sandrilene, a beautiful young girl whose heart was bound to the golden sands of her home by the sea. I longed to hear her story, and thought that maybe tonight, the magic of my name would finally be revealed to me.

"I want you to tell you something. Life ain't all it's cracked up to be. Sometimes you can't wait for the rain to stop, you gotta step outta the storm on your own." He looked at me cryptically. "You see that spot there?" he pointed to the path that led up to ES Hill's Bathing Tents pavilion. I waited, listening for some secret message I felt he was trying to impart. "I had my picture taken there this morning. It's my present to you. I want you to pick it up in a couple of days…chap who took the photo is on Baltimore Avenue—Fredericsson's his name I think."

"But Papa, why would I need a picture of you if I already have…you?" I felt a wisp of panic somewhere deep in myself, but my father whisked it away by standing up and brushing the sand off his thighs, and hoisting me up off the sand. "Time for a treat!" he proclaimed (my parents were quite skilled at ignoring the swirl of emotions that arose around me thus far in my life, and as a result, I became equally skilled at being attuned to when they were doing so).

I never told my mother of that conversation, nor did I ever let on that I'd heard her in the pantry that September afternoon. We never established a grave site for my father; when I asked her, my mother only replied, "He is where he is." Sometimes I would walk down past the beach cottages in town as far as I could towards Lewes Beach where the tourists never wandered and the cries of the gulls seemed wilder than those on Rehoboth Avenue. The cold wind-swept landscape gave me solace in the winters when I thought about my father.

The Great Storm of 1914 came to Rehoboth and everything washed away, including Horn's Pier. I was fourteen by then, no longer a child. The Great War began and the dream of going to Rehoboth was put on hold for many whose summers had always included the yearly trip to the beach. My mother and I took jobs at the Henlopen Hotel as housekeepers, making beds for the tourists who eventually came back, wiping down bathroom counters, stepping over beach towels and picking up clothes that had been tossed on the floor, even as bathing suits hung on the radiators to dry.

We pleaded with management to let us have off the week our relatives from Pennsylvania came for their yearly visit—not so much to spend time with them but because our cousins would have been horrified to learn that we were the ones cleaning up after them.

Back in the recesses of my mind, I held on to the idea that my father was still out there. My mother had ceased discussing the subject years before. At the age of eighteen, I left Rehoboth to attend Marywood College in Scranton, Pennsylvania. The Great War had just ended, and my father would have been forty-eight. One rainy afternoon, I ran into a man in Philadelphia at the Reading Terminal Market who looked like an older version of my father, selling books at one of the market stalls. My heart tumbled over when I saw him; I felt the cold shock of a disastrous truth unfolding. I had come with a friend to Philadelphia from the college for the weekend and she and I had agreed to go our separate ways in the market and meet up for lunch at one of the stalls. Terrified that he would see me, I flipped through some of the books and examined him under the guise of feigning interest in the Gardening section. My heart pounded loudly in my ears as I saw him spot me in the aisle.

He came over to me. "Do you like to garden?" His blue-grey eyes were the same. I was sure it was him. I put the book back on the shelf. "No, I'm from Rehoboth Beach, Delaware. It's hard to grow a garden by the sea." I spoke boldly, waiting for a response. My heart was thundering now. His eyes flashed; I saw a familiar light. Did he not recognize me? Yes, my hair had been blonde and curly as a child, and now it was a mousy brown, perched in a bun on the top of my head. And yes, I had grown in height and curves over the years, but surely if I were his daughter, wouldn't he have known? In disbelief, I took off my spectacles and stared at him, desperate for this man to recall who I was to him.

"Ah, Rehoboth. Been there myself. Hard to grow a garden, yes, but not impossible." His eyes cast downwards and my heart skipped a beat. I stared at him, willing him to recognize me. Perhaps too many years had passed for him to remember me as a child. "And how is Rehoboth?" he asked softly, fingering the spine of a book on perennials.

The idea that perhaps it wasn't him began to seep into my astonishment. For a moment, I considered the scar that ran from the middle of his cheekbone to his ear. My father hadn't had a scar on his face. Maybe he had fought in the Great War and been injured. Maybe—and it startled me to think this suddenly—it wasn't him.

"Well, I don't know actually. You see, I'm all grown up now and going to college. The women's college in Scranton—Marywood College, it's called. My mother, well, she still lives in Rehoboth. I plan to go back this summer to visit. Really, it's home. I'm actually looking for a book for my mother's birthday. She's quite interested in fashion. Do you have any books on fashion?" I blathered on, feeling awkward and obtuse.

He looked at me intently. Was it him? I couldn't be sure. Yes, I was quite certain he'd not had a scar on his face. And his eyes—they were kind eyes like my father's—but it seemed suddenly that they were not the eyes of the man who had named me Sandrilene in that long ago time and place.

Suddenly, the friend I'd come with appeared at my side, nudging me and saying, "There you are, I'm famished!" When I'd turned back to say goodbye to the bookseller (my father?) he had already become engaged with another customer. The moment was over, and I left, shaken.

My third year of college the dean summoned me into his office, two weeks after my mother and I realized we couldn't afford for me to continue my schooling. He spoke gravely to me as I sat in the darkened study of his office. "Someone has made a generous donation for you to continue your studies until graduation…an anonymous donor who only wishes to see you do your best in life." When I pressed him to tell me who it was, he continued, "The college has a strict policy on revealing anonymous donations. I suggest you make the most of your education and consider doing the same for another young student at some point in your own life." I never found out who my benefactor was; the situation only compounded the ever-present rock of uncertainty and confusion that had plagued me throughout the years. For many months that year, I allowed myself to believe it was the bookseller—my father—who had stepped back into my life and was watching over me from a distance. But my nascent hope diminished when no one came forth, and in the spring, my longing to find out compelled me to go back to the Market, and attempt to confront the situation once and for all.

One chilly morning in early May, I arrived anxious and breathless in the noisy and cavernous hall. Breaking into a run near the fragrant muffins and hot cross buns of the Amish Bakery, I wound my way through the desperate maze of stalls to find my father. When I saw—suddenly, precipitously—that a flower stall inhabited the former site of his books, my hope collapsed into itself. My despair was complete when I asked the dark-complexioned grocer in the neighboring stall where the bookseller had gone; his response resulted in an alarmed look and the words I was dreading, "No, miss. No, no … he gone. Many, many months ago." When I returned to school that afternoon after enduring the heavy ache of the train ride, I felt as if I had no choice but to lay aside the painful disquiet of ambiguity once more.

And so my life continued and the years passed. After I graduated from college, I married a boy from the same Pennsylvania county where my father grew up. We had two sons, and settled down for many years. Our eldest was killed on a reconnaissance mission in Germany the last year of WWII, but our second son was too young to enlist. Several years later, my mother and husband died the same year; both left a hole in my heart, but it was a hole I could fill with the certainty of grandchildren and my decision to move back to Rehoboth Beach in my old age.

It was in these later years of my life that I found it, while browsing through a pile of old photographs in the back of the used bookstore on Maryland Avenue. Vintage Photographs, read the box. The photograph lay between a picture of the old Post Office in 1910 and a group of people sitting on the beach taking off their shoes.

There he was. My father. Right there at the top of the dune next to ES Hill's Bathing Tent Pavilion, wearing a striped bathing top and boots, and holding an umbrella, next to a sign saying "Rehoboth Rink" on a beautiful, Atlantic late summer day. There was a large scratch down the middle of the photograph, marring the image. I turned it over and read in faint script, K. Fredericsson, 1910.

I realized then, not without some pain, that we see what we want to see. We have the ability to frame the moments in our lives, to take pieces of information available to us, and to create a mosaic, bit by bit, day after day, year after year to make sense of our life. My mother's refusal to honor my father's life with a gravestone and the picture that my father had promised to me the day before he disappeared were bits of this disguised narrative that, when laid bare, revealed the reality that I had been abandoned.

I understood that afternoon that Grief, in all its complexity, wears many hats. For some, Grief is a beast that attacks, plunging its victim into the cold depths of the ocean, causing panic, a gasping for air, a sudden drop into terror. For others, like me, it was not violent or destructive. Like the waves of the ocean lapping against the shore, it was a rhythmic grief, a steady presence that was carved out of the contours of my heart over years and time. My father was gone; he had left us of his own free will. My belief that the bookseller had been my father had been a blurry hope that had sustained me after the long years of missing him as a child. I understood now that I could accept the clear, sharp lines of truth. Like the photograph I held in my hand, the image of my father had stayed fixed in time, and it was time to let go.

But that was not the end of my story.

One afternoon, when I was very old and unable to walk by myself to the beach anymore, my oldest grandson, Steven, came to visit with his children. They had rolled me onto the beach in a beach chair, the kind with big wheels that could move clumsily through the sand. It was August, a lovely day on the beach, and the tourists at Rehoboth were present in full force with the detritus of a beach excursion— coolers, beach toys, towels, and aluminum chairs with sand stuck to them. We settled in a spot near the waves, among the throngs of people. The wind was blowing, the sun blazing, the tide coming in noisily as the waves crashed on the beach.

I began to doze as the bustle of settling into a beach spot surrounded me. I heard laughter, then my great-grandson Joey exclaim, "It's like the man in Grammy's picture!" My eyes flew open, and there was his father—my adult grandson Steven—in a striped T-shirt struggling to put up the beach umbrella in the sand, to give us some respite from the sun. A memory of my father holding me above the waves and singing "Sandrilene, my ocean queen" seared across miles and time into my thoughts. The realization that tiny grains of forgiveness had presented themselves to me over the years suddenly comforted me, and the memory faded.

Closing my eyes against the moment, I heard the shouting of children and insistent seagulls over the cresting of the waves, and felt the warmth of a Rehoboth summer day on my face. I knew that in a couple of hours, we would have to pack up and head home, but for now, I let Grief's cousins—joy and loneliness—greet me like old friends walking towards me on the beach, hand in hand.

8. PEOPLE ON DUNE

Photo Courtesy of Rehoboth Beach Historical Society and Museum

Shoes Off – 1914

by Sharon K. Sheppard

When starchy propriety
forbids the skin its right of sun,
the face its kiss of salt or sand,
shedding one's shoes
  must do
for toes, however craven,
may wiggle and dig
  without reproach,
sighing all day
to the wanton touch
of wind and wave.

Under the Wide Open Sky

by Alice Morris

how risqué we are
removing shoes and socking
in mixed company

Shoes Off

by Shelly Kahn

We pause and exhale
our release
from the trappings of
colder months,
our toes covered
by a sandy glaze
on this clear blue
ever forward
moving
morning.

9. BOARDWALK LADIES

Photo Courtesy of Rehoboth Beach Historical Society and Museum

Letters to My Sister on My Honeymoon, 1917

by Marjorie F. Weber

Saturday, August 4

Oh, Maddy,

I know it's my honeymoon, but I wish you could be here with me. I wish you could see what I'm seeing for the first time, the ocean, so blue against white sand, sparkling in the light, stretching on and on, it seems like forever. And the air, the first thing I noticed when I got off the train, the fresh, salt air. Without even thinking about it, I took a deep breath and suddenly, I wasn't tired anymore.

Even so, Maddy, I'm wondering what I'm doing here, still second guessing myself. I look at my new husband and I ask myself again and again what did I do? Do all new brides feel this way?

The train ride from Philadelphia took all day. The August heat was oppressive. Mostly, it was hot and dusty and long, so hot that, even with the windows open, Teddy shed his jacket and I had to take off my hat. I wish women didn't always have to wear long sleeves and long skirts. I was so hot that my petticoat stuck to my legs and my hair fell out of its chignon.

Early on, we stopped for a layover at Wilmington in Delaware and walked in the shade by the river. Teddy bought us iced coffee with cream and something I've never tasted, a circle of fried dough they rolled in powdered sugar. It was light and crisp on the outside and soft inside, heavenly.

We stopped for a second layover in Dover, about halfway there, and ate lunch in a grove of trees near the station. Mother packed a picnic of cold roast chicken, boiled eggs, biscuits, and grapes, Grandma's molasses cookies and lemonade. The lemonade was a treat, still cool, thank goodness.

Along the way, we passed these sweet little towns, so much smaller than our town, nothing more than a general store, a post office and a few charming white clapboard homes with wide porches and farmland all around. I couldn't imagine what it would be like to live there. Too quiet for me.

I kept looking at the wedding band on my finger, how the diamond caught the light, then I'd sneak a look at Teddy. Everything about him is so familiar to me. After all he's our brother George's best friend. I know him by heart: his square, open face, his wide crooked smile, how blue his eyes are, how he's always pushing his hair out of his eyes, and how this skinny kid had filled out. How easy it is to be with him. But...

Is there always a "but?"

I know I've gone and done it. After all, I'm nearly twenty-two and it's time—most of my friends are engaged or already married. And you know how Mother worried about both of us, that we'd be spinsters like Aunt Sylvie.

Still, Maddy, I can't believe I'm married. I was shaking something awful when we took our vows. You and George are so happy he's in the family. So are Mom and Dad. I wish I could be as sure.

But I wonder. Lately, I'll be going along and William will just pop up in my head. I know, I know, I shouldn't talk this way. He's been stuck in my mind ever since he stopped by the house a few weeks ago to say good-bye and wish me well before he left for West Point—he cut quite a figure in his uniform. I wish he hadn't come by. It's been a year since I broke off with him and I was okay with it. But now I wonder. My life would have been so different, Maddy. Everything feels so predictable now, nice, but predictable, working alongside of Teddy and Teddy's dad, keeping the books for the general store his family owns, having a family, living all my life in the same town, maybe in the same house.

Did I tell you William wants to move to New York City? He wants to travel too. I would have liked that, at least for a little while.

I wonder if Teddy knows I have a bad case of wanderlust. Maybe the honeymoon in Rehoboth Beach is his gift to me, his way of telling me he knows. I've always wanted to see the ocean.

A horse and buggy brought us from the station to our hotel. It's magnificent, right on the beach with a view of the ocean from almost every room. Because we're honeymooners, they're spoiling us. We have a room on the second floor right near the porch, a big room with two windows that I threw open right away to catch the sea breeze, and a sitting area with two chairs where we can sit and look out over the ocean. A stairway from the porch takes us down to a wooden boardwalk. From the boardwalk, there are steps every so often down to the beach.

I keep staring at the ocean. I've never seen anything like it.

We took an early evening stroll and passed by two daughters and their mother—at least we think they are family—carrying parasols to shield their complexions from the sun. Teddy nodded and tipped his hat and they politely nodded back. They were all so stylish, right out of the pages of *Modern Priscilla*. The mother's dress was light blue with a ruffled skirt and an embroidered silk bodice and she was wearing rings on both hands, diamond earrings and a pendant necklace. The daughters wore white lace blouses with long sleeves, high collars and lace bustle skirts, hand tailored I would guess, elegant clothes, nothing like the ready-to-wear cotton frock that I had on. Dressed like that, they can only be society.

Teddy's so funny, making up stories about them, Maddy, that they're the family of a senator, that they're summering here away from the Washington, D.C. heat, waiting for him to join them when Congress lets out in late August. I wonder who they really are, what interesting places they have been, if the daughters have fiancés waiting for them when they return home.

I wonder if they're the kind of family William will marry into.

I have to go now. Teddy made reservations for dinner. The hotel restaurant is serving oysters and crab cakes, fresh corn on the cob, and angel food cake with a whipped strawberry topping for dessert.

Sunday, August 5
I wore the navy and red bathing suit we picked out at Wanamaker's to the beach, you know, sleeveless, with the

skirt to my knees so it's not too heavy when I dunk in the water. I like the way it looks on me, although I'm not sure I can get used to walking around with bare legs. Teddy tells me all the time that he likes brunettes with brown eyes like mine and curly hair, even when I tell him I wish I had straight hair like yours. This morning, he gave me a little pat on the bottom. "Pretty," he said with a shy smile. I couldn't help but giggle.

Teddy and I are so close, you know, in a nice way. I'm blushing. Ladies don't talk about these things. Enough said.

On the beach, I went in the ocean up to my knees, but not any further because my bathing suit is wool and when it gets wet, it gets too heavy. I can't really swim anyway. Teddy stood right by, his hand in mine, steadying me against the waves coming in. Later, he left me to swim out with some of the other men just beyond where the waves were breaking. I wish I could swim out there with him.

Oh Maddy, I'm still nervous. I think, this is it. I've gone and done it.

Did you have second thoughts when you got married? I expected something else, the way all my friends talk. I expected to be swept off my feet. And what I feel is comfortable, just the way I did before, when he was always around.

I mean this was the boy who was my big brother's best friend, who used to pull my pigtails and tease me endlessly about anything, about the gap in my smile when I lost my tooth, about the cookies I burned, about a tear in my stocking. Anything. He used to make me so mad.

But then, he's family—how many times have you and Mother told me that? I know, I know, he was the one who found my kitten when she was lost. He was the one who always jumped up to help Mom with the groceries, who got us all up from dinner to play Kick the Can summer evenings at dusk, who had the courage to climb to the top branch of our apple tree to grab those hard-to-reach apples, who helped me climb to the first branch and steadied me when I was afraid I'd fall. He was my first crush when I was ten. He was always there.

I guess I expected some boy to appear out of nowhere and dazzle me, someone like William.

Did I tell you, it wasn't until William started calling on me and dropped by the General Store that Teddy started coming around all formal and serious and I figured out he was courting me? I didn't take him seriously until he asked me to marry him and told me to choose between him and William. I was surprised when he told me he had always loved me.

But then, you and Mother told me if I didn't say yes, Ada Jackson might walk away with him and Mary O'Hare had her eye on him too. I wasn't ready yet, but all my girlfriends were engaged or had gotten married already and, the truth was and still is, I couldn't imagine not having him in my life.

So I closed my eyes and jumped.

Maddy, I shouldn't have written this. Please burn it after you finish reading it.

Wednesday, August 8
We're going fishing today. If we catch anything, the chef at the hotel restaurant said he'll cook it for our dinner.

Teddy asks so many questions. I like his curiosity, how he wants to know everything—the history of this place, what type of fish they catch here, how some of the local people came to be here. We still see the mother and her two daughters we passed by on the boardwalk. They have a suite with a private porch on the first floor of our hotel where they spend most of their time. When they do come to the dining room, they sit by themselves at the same table by a corner window at every meal and talk only to each other. They seemed so sad somehow, even here in this beautiful place, that we stopped making up stories about them.

I worry that I'm getting too much sun. My face is getting tan even though I wear a sunhat. But I can't stay away from the beach. I love the sound of the tide washing up along the shoreline and the cry of seagulls as they swoop in to snatch a fish from the water. I love the smell of the sea and the taste of salt on my lips and walking by the water's edge and discovering shells in the wet sand. Yesterday, I found two conches, one white and long and curvy, the other brown with a pink inside. I can't wait to show you.

It's so lazy and peaceful here, you can float through the day.

Friday, August 10
Today we were on the beach when, out of nowhere, the wind came up and clouds rolled in, big black clouds, stacked one on top of another, coming in so fast we barely had time to collect our things and run before the rain fell. It rained for hours, Maddy. You should have seen the ocean, so black

and angry and the tide coming up higher than I'd ever seen it, halfway up the beach.

They said it was a nor'easter that came off the ocean and up the coast. No one knew it was coming. They can't always predict storms here.

Teddy and I, we huddled together on the second story porch. I was a little scared but he was just riveted by the beauty of it, the wildness we were witnessing. We stayed there until the hotel staff began pulling chairs inside and shuttering windows against the gale.

When the tide came up to the boardwalk, the staff ran up and down the hallways, ringing Maritime Bells, shouting for us to pack an overnight bag and meet in the lobby. Just as quickly, the horse and buggy that took us from the railroad station to the hotel pulled up to the entrance and we piled in, riding to the firehouse where they were putting up dozens of tourists like us.

After he safely deposited me, while all of us claimed our small patch of space on the floor of the garage, Teddy rolled up his sleeves and rode back to the hotel with the staff to collect food and blankets and hurricane lamps for the stay here. A few men took his lead, followed after him. But most stayed.

I looked around the room but couldn't find them. "Teddy, our ladies aren't here," I told him the next time he came in. By this time, I was worried. "I'll look for them," he said as he turned to leave.

I pitched in, helping to prepare food as best we could. There was very little, some leftover bread from lunch, boxed cereal and canned goods the hotel staff brought in. We had meat and fish but no way to cook it—the firewood was soaked. They brought bottles of fresh water that had been stashed away for emergencies like this one, but we were rationed—no one knew how long the storm would last. People were hungry and tired and scared.

Maddy, the rain pounded the roof and the wind shook the walls so hard I expected the building to collapse around us. I kept watching the door, waiting, it seemed like hours, imagining that Teddy had been swept away by the tide that had already swallowed the boardwalk and was flooding the road just above where we were staying.

Finally the three of them came in through the door, the mother and her two daughters, all of them soaked to the skin, and Teddy right behind them, his arm on the mother's elbow to steady her against the wind. I cleared out a space for them on the wall by me, wrapped dry blankets around them and brought them cold tea and sandwiches before I walked Teddy to the door.

He told me the mother, Mrs. Winters, was huddled, terrified, on her trunk in the corner of the room farthest from the windows even as high tide brought the water up to the porch in front of their suite. The hotel staff could not persuade her to go without her things, even when the daughters begged her to leave. Everyone was frantic.

I don't know what Teddy said to her, but here they all were, in the firehouse, without her trunk but safe, and Mrs. Winters was thanking me again and again for Teddy's help.

And I thought then of how he is in his father's store, always pleasant to the customers, rarely ruffled, always able to find an answer to any problem they bring to him. I surprise myself that I hadn't noticed that before. But then, I hadn't been looking, had I, Maddy?

The storm kept on. Teddy stopped by the firehouse every hour or so to check up on me and then go out again. I watched him heft boxes of food, help the men clear debris from the road and I marveled at how calm, how competent he was in the midst of the chaos in the storm's aftermath. He and the other men were already on a first name basis. Crisis will do that.

Saturday, August 11
Everything came to a halt.

There were maybe fifty people squeezed into this space, a baby, a few toddlers, and a few families among them. The baby whimpered, his brothers and sisters, still in bathing suits, shivered and squirmed as they clung to their weary mother, her back against a side wall. She stroked the girl's hair and wrapped a damp blanket more tightly around them. There was nothing much else she could do.

Restless, elegantly dressed tourists sat or stood, moved around the cramped room, stepped outside for a bit of fresh air, and returned, pushed back inside by the still wild winds. In the dim light, an older woman, thin, wearing glasses, her hat still properly in place, intently read a book she had brought with her. A group of men gathered in a back room and silently played cards. Faces drawn and gray, the people gathered in this room said very little. This was a waiting game.

I ached with fatigue, felt suddenly fragile. My blouse and skirt were damp and dirty, my stockings torn, my hair knotted. When I was not fixing or serving food, I dozed standing or sitting with my legs tucked under me in the small space next to Mrs. Winters.

All I wanted was to go home. Everyone did.

Teddy came in and out with the other men, checking on me, stopping, taking my hand, bending to pat me on the cheek. When the storm raged, he would come in and stay until it subsided, then he was out again. They were rescuing stragglers now, people who didn't make it to shelter earlier, hurrying before the next high tide brought in more flooding. I was always looking toward the door. Staying busy with food or making people more comfortable, if that was even possible, was the only way I kept from thinking. When I wasn't afraid of how the wind shook the walls, how the rain pounded the windows or whether the building would collapse around us, I was worrying that Teddy would not come back to me, that the storm would take him. But he always came back.

His steadiness calmed me in a way I had not imagined. I had forgotten how our family and his depended on him for the littlest things, a lost kitten, a loose shingle, a pick up baseball game, another hand to bring in groceries. Sometimes, you don't see what's standing right there in front of you, Maddy.

If I weren't so tired and we could be alone, I would tell him how proud I am of him, of the way he took charge, the way he worked so well alongside men who were strangers before today. I would tell him he made me feel safe. I'll tell him when we get home.

In the afternoon, the storm cleared out and we saw a patch of sun before a few clouds rolled in again. It was a bad storm, not the worst, local people said with relief, they have lived through worse, much worse. There was damage, more than I have ever seen from a storm, but only a few injuries, nothing serious, and no deaths. Teddy told me the main road was washed out and littered with tree branches, and whole sections of the boardwalk were gone. Winds tipped someone's Model T on its side. The men working at our hotel told us the first floor had been flooded and the porch on a hotel down the block from ours was ripped off.

We build our lives with such confidence, but I am struck now by how fragile everything really is. I was wrong about a life being predictable.

Monday, August 13
The water receded. The wealthy among us found money to pay local people to collect their trunks from the hotels and cart them to the train station. The road is clear enough now so they can pick their way through the muck and the downed trees to get to the station. They say trains are expected to run again any minute, but none have come yet. I heard that a few hired horse-drawn buggies to take them to Dover beyond where the tracks have washed out, Mrs. Winters and her daughters among them.

Before she left, she sought me out. "Be sure to thank your wonderful husband for me," she said as she pulled from her hair a pearl and diamond barrette and pressed it into my palm. "He's a kind man. I hope my daughters will be so lucky."

And as I stood there and held that barrette in my hand and watched her go, I knew that I had never really seen Teddy like this before, not the way you and Mother do, the way Mrs. Winters does.

Because Teddy pitched in, Martha and Paul Clark who live here year-round offered us a spare bedroom in their home five blocks from the beach, untouched by the flooding. We gratefully accepted. Someone, a saint I think, retrieved my trunk. I washed from a bucket of warmed rain water, changed clothes and slept soundly for the first time since the storm came in. Teddy stopped only to clean up and eat, then he was gone again, off with the men to clear side roads.

There are fewer people at the firehouse now. Martha and I cooked at her home and returned with food. She brought dry wool blankets for the children.

Tuesday, August 14
The Clarks had a friend who brought us by buggy up to Dover, no charge. Some of the men Teddy worked with gathered with the Clarks to see us off.

We said good-bye, promised to write. I know we'll come back here, see them again but it will be different, better, because we know so many people.

The oppressive August heat has returned but the train ride was easy this time. I set my head on Teddy's shoulder and nodded off; he woke me up for the Wilmington layover where we treated ourselves to fried dough and iced coffee again. I have begun to feel normal.

I told Teddy Mrs. Winters sent her thanks and showed him the exquisite barrette she had given me. And we marveled that, distracted by the fury of the storm, we had learned little more about her and her daughters than we had when we first noticed them. I closed my hand around the barrette and smiled, thought of how I will always remember her, not for the barrette, but for her words: "A kind man. I hope my daughters will be so lucky."

As the train slowed coming into the Philadelphia station, Teddy took my hand, leaned toward me and whispered, "I love you."

I don't wonder anymore if I made the right choice. I squeezed his hand, smiled, and whispered back, "I love you too." But he didn't hear me. He was already standing in the aisle of our car, his hand on the baggage rack to steady himself against the rock of the train, gathering our luggage as the train, brakes squealing, slowed coming into the Philadelphia Station. And home.

No matter. There will be time for saying that again. A lifetime.

Seaside Footsteps

by Mary Ellen South

They walked the promenade
Skirts swishing, conversation high
Parasols protecting from the sun
The sea's soft symphony paced their steps.

They walk the boards
Sandals and shorts, rap voices
Sunscreen protects their tattooed bodies
The sea's soft symphony ignored.

History's seaside attraction
forever the gathering place.

Mary Ellen South

10. WADING

Photo Courtesy of Rehoboth Beach Historical Society and Museum

Man in a Straw Boater

by Jack Mackey

Death, faceless, exposed
double, spectral vision, he
sits dryly, chooses.

11. PORCH

Photo Courtesy of Rehoboth Beach Historical Society and Museum

Katie Finds Her Voice

by Nancy Powichroski Sherman

Katie Sullivan leaned her back against Mrs. Mahoney's oak tree and fluttered a paper fan over her face, trying to cool her warm cheeks. Though she would be home earlier than the required time, she was anxious and fearful that the blush that spread across her face might arouse suspicion and, if questioned about what she had been doing all afternoon, her hesitation would proclaim guilt, though she had done nothing wrong. Truly.

"Hey, Katie!" The squeaky pitch of her younger cousin Lenny's voice cut though the summer day like a balloon with its air being squeezed out. He clanged the tin bell on his bicycle as he pedaled toward her and skidded to a stop. "Whatcha doin'?"

She certainly didn't need a nosey annoyance at this moment. "Nothing, Lenny." She folded her fan and slipped it into her purse.

The little pest jumped off his bicycle and dropped it on the grass. "Then why are ya just standin' here?" He pointed down the street. "Yer mom 'n dad are on the front porch. Looks like they're drinkin' some of that sweet tea yer mom makes." He waved his arms in their direction. "Hey, Aunt Thelma! Hey, Uncle Robert!"

Katie stopped her cousin's arms in mid-wave. "You go get some of that tea, Lenny. I'll be there in a minute."

"Ya waitin' for somebody?"

She crossed her eyes at him. "No, I am not. I'm just catching my breath after a long walk."

"Where'd ya go?"

"Around the world, okay?" Just then, the steeple bell from St. Agnes-by-the-Sea Catholic Church started its hourly bell sequence. "Four o'clock. Isn't that when you're due home for dinner? You'd best get moving before your momma counts those bells." Lenny's mother was her Aunt Alice who rented the smaller bungalow behind the cottage where Katie's family spent their summers.

Her cousin was back on his bike and pedaling furiously before the fourth bell completed its vibrations.

As Katie resumed her walk to the summer cottage, she focused her thoughts on topics that would seem natural as dinner table conversation. She could tell her parents about the morning meeting at the church hall and that, being sixteen-almost-seventeen, she was the youngest volunteer this summer. She could tell them about the craft boxes that she and the other volunteers prepared for next week's Catholic Youth Camp. And she could relate a joke the pastor had made about Moses parting the sea. Anything but what happened after the camp meeting when she took a stroll on the boardwalk and met someone who was new to Rehoboth, a young woman her own age of sixteen who, like Katie, was looking for a summer friend. If only the new girl, Nettie, weren't the niece of William and Elizabeth Gilmore, the couple whose oceanfront summer home, Seaside Retreat, was large enough to be a hotel. Katie's father disapproved of the casual attitude of that family, whom he declared loud and extravagant. So, in recounting the events of the day, she couldn't dare mention the new dresses in the window of the general store because she might accidentally mention that Nettie had walked right in and bought one on credit.

As she approached the cottage, a sigh of relief slipped out when she saw that her parents were indeed on the porch—her mother embroidering a handkerchief and her father immersed in a new hardback book, its dust cover removed and carefully laid on the side table far from his half-empty glass of sweet tea. With both her parents occupied, they might not engage her in a conversation.

No such luck. Her father looked up from reading. "How was the camp meeting, Kathleen? Was there a good turnout this year?"

"Yes, Father. Mrs. Longfellow is pleased that we'll have enough camp leaders for each age group and still have an extra one in case someone gets ill." Hoping to steer the conversation, she tipped her head to look at the book her father held. "This Side of Paradise by F. Scott Fitzgerald. Is he a new author?"

"Indeed, but the newspapers say that he shows promise as a novelist. The postman delivered it this morning." He marked the page with the needlework bookmark she had made for him. "It's the story of how shallow the younger generation is as they pursue pleasure rather than put shoulder-to-the-wheel and contribute to the betterment of this world."

She noticed that her mother had stopped the embroidery needle halfway through a stitch and was studying her face. "What's wrong, Momma?"

Before an answer could be given, Katie's father asked, "Where did you go after you left the church hall?"

Katie willed her cheeks to not turn red, but the flush spread too quickly for her to stop it. "The sky is so beautiful today that I couldn't help but take a long walk."

"By yourself?"

Katie didn't dare raise her eyes. "No. With a friend."

"A friend? And who would that be?"

"A new friend, actually." Every bit of moisture seemed to dry up in her mouth and make speaking difficult. "Her name is Nettie." Her father waited for her to complete the name. "Nettie Gilmore. She's staying with her uncle and aunt this summer."

He gently wrapped his book in the dust cover, smoothing the edges to perfection. "Kathleen, you know that I do not approve of your spending any time with people like them. Remember the maxim: *Associate yourself with people of good quality, if you esteem your own reputation; for it is better to be alone than in bad company.*"

"Yes, Father." She wanted to counter his quote with *Judge not, that ye be not judged*, but she didn't dare.

"Don't ever lie to me again, Kathleen."

"I haven't lied, Father."

"You avoided telling us about Nettie; I had to draw it out of you. You know that concealing information is a form of lie. What do we call that sin?"

Katie's face burned so intensely that she could swear that the gates of Hell opened and were awaiting her fall. "The sin of omission."

Her mother laid the embroidery hoop on the side table, never taking her eyes off her daughter, but said nothing until her husband left the porch. "Katie, be careful. Your Aunt Alice saw you with Nettie. You know she shares your father's opinion of the Gilmores."

"But, Momma, Nettie shouldn't be assumed bad, based solely on her relatives."

"Agreed. But you must consider your father's point of view. He's only thinking of you and of your future. It's important to him that you present yourself as wholesome and appropriate." She patted her daughter's hand. "Surely you can find friendship among the counselors at the camp."

"They're old and married and boring. I have nothing in common with them. I finally have someone my own age to be a friend, even if just a summer friend, and father won't allow it." She rushed to her bedroom and dramatically threw herself across the chenille bedspread. Summer stretched before her like a prison sentence; she may as well have stayed in Philadelphia despite the sweltering heat.

Her disappointment turned to thoughts of rebellion, however tempered by the reality that her father was the head of the family and ruled accordingly. If she couldn't enjoy the summer with Nettie, then she'd quit the youth camp and cloister herself here on the second floor where she could at least find adventure in reading the novels she brought from home. Perhaps she would alert her parents to her despondence by refusing dinner tonight.

The longer she daydreamed about her strategies, the less possible they seemed. And the more childish. When called downstairs to dinner, her plans dissolved into a great white emptiness.

The following morning, she returned to St. Agnes-by-the-Sea for another day of preparing craft boxes for the upcoming camp activities, but her heart and mind were elsewhere. She wondered what Nettie might be doing. Perhaps she was sleeping late. Or having her breakfast on the wrap-around porch at her uncle's beach house. Or whatever wealthy people do in the morning.

Her sighs led Mrs. Longfellow to ask, "Are you ill, Kathleen?"

"Maybe. I'm feeling a little under the weather." It was a tiny fib on her conscience, but the reward was an unexpected emancipation when Mrs. Longfellow suggested that she take the rest of the day off.

She took slow, deliberate steps as she left the church property, mostly for appearance, but also using the time to weigh her desire to seek out Nettie versus fear that her father would find out. But when she turned the corner, the decision was made and her stride matched her zeal as she hurried south toward Lake Charles, arriving at the Gilmore summer residence before the church bells finished ringing the Angelus.

Seaside Retreat seemed more beautiful than ever with the sun sending flashes of diamond-light across the blue tin roof and bouncing off the glass that formed the inlaid mosaics of the stone patio. Under a canvas canopy, a table holding a vase with fresh flowers and recently used tableware awaiting removal gave her hope that Nettie would suddenly appear.

But, when the door opened, it was a woman dressed in a maid's uniform.

Katie summoned her courage to ask, "Is Nettie at home?"

The woman's nod was unnecessary as Nettie, dressed in a striped bathing suit, appeared on the second floor porch. "Katie!" She skipped down the steps and, taking Katie's hand, led her to the ocean side of the house. "What a marvelous coincidence. I was just wishing that you were here, and suddenly you are." She gestured toward two young men reclining on deck chairs. "I'd like you to meet Alan Jansen and Teddy Peterson."

Katie's smile froze on her face. What if she were seen here, not just with Nettie, but also with two men? Her inclination was to leave immediately, but when the young men rose to greet her and offered the chairs to Nettie and her, while they themselves sat on the sand, their chivalry and handsome faces convinced her that staying was indeed the proper choice. After all, she'd been raised to be polite. And, before the bells from the church chimed four o'clock, Katie had enjoyed listening to Alan's and Teddy's stories of university life, had noticed that blue-eyed Teddy looked more in her direction than in Nettie's, and had been invited to join the three of them at Horn's Motion Picture Theatre that evening as a double-date.

When she was leaving the Retreat, she confided in Nettie that her father might not allow her to attend the show.

Nettie's eyebrows furrowed. "Why not?"

Katie wouldn't admit that her father did not approve of the Gilmores or that he'd forbidden any friendship with

Nettie. Instead, she said, "He's old fashioned about court-ship."

"Old fashioned? Does he still insist on chaperones? Tell him that you'll be with a Gilmore; that should solve every-thing."

Katie pretended to accept Nettie's advice and agreed, with as much resolve as she could muster, that she'd ask permission to attend the movie.

As she rushed back to the summer cottage, she was in a terror of "what-ifs." What if someone saw her near Lake Charles? What if Mrs. Longfellow had stopped by the cot-tage to check on her?

It was imperative that Katie introduce the topic of her brief hiatus from camp duties and supply enough details to seem transparent. "The heat was stifling today and the church hall unbearable. Mrs. Longfellow kindly excused me early from camp so I could get some ocean air. But I feel better now."

"You're still a bit flushed." Her mother poured her a glass of sweet tea. "Sit out here with us for a while. There's a nice breeze coming through."

Katie willed her pounding heart to calm while her brain raced for how she might reveal the whole story, thereby avoiding another sin of omission, and yet still get permission to see the show that night.

But Aunt Alice ruined everything by appearing with Len-ny in tow. "Robert!"

Immediately, Katie's chest tightened as she waited for the ax to fall, but her aunt's grip on Lenny removed her worries.

"Would you like a son? He needs a strong man to set him right. Since Howard passed on, this youngster seems to think himself independent and disappears any time work needs to be done." If she weren't so angry at Lenny, her Aunt Alice's eyes would have filled as they always did when she spoke of her husband who had died in the war.

"But, Ma, this is summer vacation."

Aunt Alice smacked his head. "Just for you? You think your mother doesn't deserve a vacation, too?"

"Ma, somebody'll take my bike if I don't go back for it."

"You won't be needing a bike anymore until you get into that cottage and clean your room. It stinks like a skunk!"

Katie's father stood up, giving him the appearance of a giant towering over his nephew. "You heard your mother, Leonard. Scoot!"

With face red and tears streaming down his cheeks, Lenny ran back to the bungalow.

Katie knew in that instant that she was not strong enough to complete her story or to broach the subject of going to the show and that she needed to get that information to Nettie immediately. "Aunt Alice, I'll retrieve his bicycle for you."

"Now that's how a good child acts." Her aunt smiled at her. "It's on the edge of the beach where he dropped it. Probably going to rust from salt air if he doesn't take better care of it."

As Katie stepped off the porch steps, she heard her mother say, "Katie, don't dawdle. Your aunt and cousin are going to join us for dinner tonight." With this extra dread added to her already sunken feeling, she headed to the beach. Her Aunt Alice's words, *That's how a good child acts*, tapped on her conscience. She didn't feel like a good child, nor did she feel like a worthy friend for Nettie.

She located the bicycle and pedaled to Seaside Retreat. Relieved that the young men had left, she sat on the empty beach chair beside Nettie's. "I can't come to Horn's to-night."

Nettie's smile struggled to stay in place. "But Teddy's expecting you. And I am, too."

"It's a family situation."

Her friend nodded toward the child's bicycle. "Did someone get hurt?"

"No. My father just won't let me go to the show."

"Why not?"

"Like I've already told you, he's strict about my social life."

Nettie's eyes widened. "Is your dad living in the dark? You're not a kid. You're almost seventeen. Girls our age are getting ready to go to college and live independently on campus where no one will make decisions for them. When are your parents going to cut the umbilical cord?"

"My father is only thinking of my future."

"In the meantime, he controls everything about you. Does he treat your mom this way, too?"

"No."

"Are you sure?" Nettie's hands settled on her hips. "My mom will vote at the next election. Will yours?"

Katie was embarrassed. Whenever the topic of the 19th amendment was mentioned, both her father and her aunt spoke vehemently against it. Her mother seldom contributed to the discussion, but Katie always assumed that her mother wasn't interested in politics. "She'll vote if she wants."

"Or not. In the meantime, my mom is dedicating her life to guarantee women's rights." Nettie shrugged. "I don't know how Teddy will react to his disappointment, but I'll think of something that doesn't make you sound like an overprotected baby."

"Nettie, please don't be mad at me." She wiped a tear from her cheek with the back of her hand.

"Stop crying, for Pete's sake." Nettie handed her a towel. "It's just a date, and Teddy's just a guy. But he's a good one, so don't make him wait too long. He's a catch, and if you hesitate, some other girl will reel him in."

Dinner was more quiet than usual. Other than the clink of forks against plates, there were only occasional comments about the July heat and the tasty meal. During a particularly long silence, a question that had been unmercifully tapping on Katie's brain spilled from her mouth before she could stop it with a forkful of mashed potatoes. "Why don't you like Nettie Gilmore?"

It was as though she had exploded a bomb. Her aunt dropped a biscuit, splashing gravy over the tablecloth. Her father laid his fork on his plate and wiped his hands with a napkin. Her mother stopped passing the bowl of peas. The only happy face was that of her cousin Lenny who saw this moment as taking the attention away from him.

Aunt Alice glared across the table. "What a question! For your information…"

But her father took over. "The Gilmores are wealthy liberals who would see the world turn upside-down. Her mother is a troublemaker, running around the country pushing for women's suffrage."

Her aunt added, "I hear that the girl is staying here for the summer because her mother is in jail again. That's what happens when you make trouble."

The rest of the dinner was spirited chatter between her father, who complained about political disorder, and her aunt, who created a wild story about imprisonment, hunger strikes, and loose women. The big finale, however, was when her father asked her if she had been in contact with Nettie. When she told the truth, her cousin Lenny let out a big whoop and finished his meal with joy.

"You will not see her again, Katie."

Deep inside, she heard her prison door slam and lock.

That night, Katie didn't sleep well. She struggled with the balance between justice and obedience. How could she let Nettie know her father's directive if she was already forbidden to see her?

The next day, while Katie was listlessly counting out crayons for the craft boxes at the church, Mrs. Longfellow asked her to run to the general store to pick up construction paper that had been ordered. On the way back, she heard her name called, and her heart sank.

"I'm sorry about the movie," Katie said with clear remorse.

Nettie waved her hand as though erasing a sentence. "No need to apologize. That's not why I've been looking for you. This morning, my uncle told me we're having special company at Seaside Retreat. Irene Castle, the dancer! She's here to perform at a charity event at the Henlopen Hotel. And it gets better: My uncle has tickets for me and you, as well as for Alan and Teddy. Isn't that…?" Katie's face surely communicated her father's declaration because Nettie stopped midsentence. "Certainly your father won't forbid you attending a charity fundraiser, especially when Irene Castle is the special guest? It's a once-in-a-lifetime experience."

Katie no longer wanted to hide behind half-truths; it was time to be honest by addressing her father's disapproval of a friendship with Nettie. "Is it true that your mother is in jail?"

"What? No. She's on a lecture tour for the Junior League and helping organize chapters of the National Women's Party. Who told you that my mom was in jail?"

"My aunt."

"Is that why you couldn't go to the motion pictures with me?"

Katie nodded. "I was wrong about my father. He's more than old-fashioned; he's close-minded. He's against change and disapproves of anyone who aims to make it happen."

"And your mom?"

Another admission of truth. "I don't know. She doesn't speak against him."

Nettie clasped Katie's forearms. "This is the 20th century, and change is going to happen regardless of your father's desire to stop time. Your mom may endure his tyranny, Katie, but when will you find your own voice?"

Her face burned at the deserved reproach. "When I'm ready."

Nettie released her hold. "Don't wait too long. As my mom says, Life will pass you by. To which I add, so will friendships and opportunities."

Katie delivered the package to Mrs. Longfellow and then, after resigning from her position at the camp, continued a steady gait until she reached the cottage.

Her mother and aunt were hanging laundry in the backyard but paused when they saw her. "Aunt Alice, I need to speak with my mother alone."

But her aunt didn't budge. "There's nothing you need to hide from me."

Her mother asked, "What's wrong, Katie?"

"Nothing's wrong." She grabbed a handful of clothespins and helped her mother secure a bed sheet to the clothesline.

Her mother tossed a leftover clothespin back into the pin bag. "Alice, would you go in and prepare the sweet tea for this afternoon?" Her obvious intention sent her sister-in-law flouncing into the main cottage.

"Momma, do you agree with father's stance on women's suffrage?"

"What is this all about, Katie?"

"Are you going to vote next year?"

"I haven't thought about it one way or the other."

"Well, I plan to vote as soon as I'm of age."

Her mother smiled. "Of course, you will. I never doubted it."

"And I think I'm old enough to choose my own friends, and even to go on a date. After all, I'm older than you were when you married father."

"You're not involved with some boy, are you? You've been acting very secretive lately."

"No, Momma. I'm not 'involved' with anyone. But I'm old enough to date, right?" She hoped for a sign from her mother, but didn't wait. "Nettie introduced me to a fine young man who wishes to court me. His name is Teddy Peterson, and he's a junior at Princeton."

"I was hoping that you would go to college, too, and become something more than a Mrs."

"Of course, I will. But I have immediate hopes, too, Momma. I want to be more independent, and it's my hope that you'll speak up for me if father refuses to budge on that issue."

"Katie, it's not my voice that counts. It's yours. Your father will treat you as an adult when you make him see that you are one."

The back door opened, and Katie's father emerged with Katie's aunt. "Kathleen, you're home early."

"Father, I have exciting news to share with you and mother. While I was running an errand for Mrs. Longfellow, Nettie approached me…"

"I have forbidden you to socialize with that young woman."

Her aunt nodded at him. "I told you that Katie was up to something."

Katie remained strong. "I didn't seek her out; she sought me with an invitation to attend a charitable event, featuring Irene Castle, at the Henlopen Hotel, courtesy of her uncle."

"Her uncle? William Gilmore?"

"Yes. William and Elizabeth Gilmore are sponsoring the fundraiser to support the efforts of the American Red Cross. Isn't that a worthy cause?"

His jaw tightened. "Worthy? They think it will earn them the respect that money alone can't buy. Well, not mine! I won't have my daughter connected with the Gilmores. Katie, you do not have my permission to attend that event."

Katie stood tall. "I didn't ask for your permission." She expected her father to take action—to slap her for her insolence, or to send her to her room, or to tell her to pack her bags for a bus back to Pennsylvania.

But he did nothing. He just stood there with his mouth slightly parted in expectation of words that hadn't formed quite yet.

Katie's knees shook a bit as she struggled to keep her resolve. But it was too late to take it back. She had opened Pandora's box and would never let it close again.

Her aunt stepped between them. "Robert, are you going to let her talk to you like that?"

When he didn't answer her, Aunt Alice stormed past and into her bungalow.

Katie felt her mother's hand touch her shoulder and heard her mother say, "Robert, Kathleen will need a new dress."

12. POST OFFICE

Photo Courtesy of Rehoboth Beach Historical Society and Museum

Hearing Is Believing

by Kathleen L. Martens

I'd long ago stopped wondering how flaming logs that snuggled in the charred stone fireplace sounded. Instead, I'd learned to lose myself in the fire's penetrating heat, its dancing colors, the sweetness of the smoke swirls of applewood that scent my hair. But ever since the postcard arrived yesterday from Father's cousin George I began to wonder again—wonder about the crackling sound, the snapping of the kindling. Today, I sit in our parlor at tea time delighting in the fire's comfort on this chilly, New England spring day, and I reach into my imagination to translate the sounds of the blaze into my soundless world.

I sip Earl Grey wearing my stylish, silver-blue tea gown I just bought in Paris on our annual house of fashion spring fling. It's lusciously loose at the bodice, with a flowing train, and without the high collar, I feel somewhat naughty, exposed. Mother had resisted the modern purchase, but with *La Mode* magazine to guide her, fashion had won out. As my British cousin, Emma, had said at the House-of-Worth-Salon-de-Vente, "It's 1910, Edwardian times now; Queen Victoria's long gone."

My back is cool against the upholstered chair while I warm my feet in new cream, high-button shoes, laced up like a corset, with a lovely silk bow on the toe. I'm pensive about the postcard, but my peace is about to be disturbed.

Mother crosses the Persian carpet, centers herself on a large burgundy flower, and rubs her hands in front of the blaze. I can predict what's coming from the pleading stance of her body, her facial expression. "Read again please, Grace."

I sign the words of the memorized message.

Postmark April 15, 1910. Rehoboth Beach, Delaware

Dearest Grace: We hope this finds you well. Tragically, Anna's fevers have now taken her hearing, permanently. She is quite disturbed to be trapped in a silent world. Would you take pity and summer with us to help your cousin? You've done so well with your situation, and as a teacher. Good cheers to your mother and my dear brother, Charles.

Affectionately, Uncle George.

"How insulting. You, *trapped* in a silent world? And your *situation?* What *situation?*" Her hands sign emphatically. "George is so ignorant... Grace, the Hearing world won't be easy. Your life here in Chilmark on The Vineyard's so perfect." Mother's words threaten my plans.

I gaze at the postcard's boardwalk photo, dozens of people strolling, women with parasols, casual long white cotton blouses and skirts cinched at the waist, their arms hooked to the arms of gentlemen in straw hats, no jackets. So free. The ocean water lifts in a suspended arc beside the strip of sand. My beloved Atlantic shore. Why can't I navigate one summer in Delaware? We sign our way through Paris every year, and fill our steamer chests with fashion and frocks.

"Are you listening?" Mother asks with flowing hands.

I'm *deaf,* how could I be *listening,* I want to say, but I keep my hands silent in my lap. Sarcasm is so inappropriate, but sometimes... I glance out the window so as not to hear her.

I know the lecture's coming. The unique history of my island village in Massachusetts, nearly everyone deaf like me. Even the Hearing speak American Sign Language.

"Cousin Anna's newly deaf. I'm a Deaf teacher; how can I not go? My own blood." I spell the word teacher, emphatically, letter by letter, when I could have used a one-word sign. Now I'm being outright ill-mannered.

Mother turns my chin so I have to watch what she is signing. "Fortunately for you, Grace Lambert, our Chilmark community on Martha's Vineyard has given you a life of normalcy," she says with punctuating signs. She repeats what I already know, our oppressed ancestors came from Kent County, England with hundreds of Deaf in 1690 having been treated as disabled, marginalized, unaccepted. They sought a new community of Deaf in America where being a part of the Deaf community defined them as much as being American. Imagine, even town meetings were conducted in Sign. Mother would always fit that in.

Does she think I have no memory as well as no hearing?

"The schools for Deaf you attended protected you." I watch Mother finish her rant, "only here do Deaf people feel they're fully accepted as…"

"Yes, Mother, I know, accepted as normal. And I am grateful." I imagine how lost my little thirteen-year-old cousin must feel joining our soundless world, adapting to her own Hearing world where she no longer fits in, they no longer see her as normal, even though she will still be able to speak. Mother means well, but my heart is tender right now, and I'm so agitated of late.

I want it; I want the adventure, to get away after my unfortunate affair with James. His disloyalty still stings. A Deaf fiancé doesn't guarantee your heart won't break, and of course, at nearly twenty-five years old, the word *spinster* is shadowing me in the gossiping hands of neighbors every day. Mother's hoping for a new match for me this summer, before I shrivel up and it's too late, I saw her tell Father.

With empty tea cup, I stare out the window at the lone oak tree perched on Chilmark Pond, watch a wavering vee of Canadian Geese passing over the marshy grasses, and shards of afternoon light flashing through clouds on the ocean beyond. My one brief childhood visit to Rehoboth still lingers, the same Atlantic Ocean from Uncle George's wrap-around porch, gulls scattering. My heart flutters with fear and excitement at the thought of living an entire summer in the foreign culture of the Hearing world. Wouldn't that discomfort make me a better teacher? It's a rare opportunity, to help a cousin, to see what fiber I am made of, perhaps. Mother fears I'm vulnerable, having been "cast aside" by James, as she calls our break-up, and I might become entangled with a Hearing man; I have no such desire; I stand firm on that. We've seen too many intercultural matches go wrong.

Despite Mother's objections, Father is in favor. He secures permission from the School Board and makes the arrangements with Uncle George. Cousin Emma is willing to accompany me. Mother is out-voted. Emma and I will leave in mid-May. Reluctantly, Mother agrees. I am sure to make peace with her before my departure.

"I love you, dear. Travel safely." She kisses my cheek as we leave the house.

As I pack my things, I dream of perambulating along the boardwalk, teaching young Anna to communicate in new ways. It will be an arduous task.

In the Pullman car on the Pennsy from Boston to Philadelphia with Emma, I have my first taste of anxiety. Can I convince my uncle and aunt they too need to learn American Sign Language? Reading lips is so ineffective, and challenging. Anna will need all modes. But unlike me, Cousin Anna has spent her entire young life speaking. Her parents will want her to pass as a Hearing person, obscure her *tragic disability*. They will not want her to be part of the Deaf culture and community. I embrace my Deaf culture, my deafness. Will they understand I don't feel I have a *tragic situation*? Being deaf is a part of who I am; I'm respected, and respectably attractive, some have said.

Cousin Emma sits beside me. So opposite, so different. She can hear; I am deaf. She's tall; I'm petite. Emma's unfashionably thin, like a plank; I'm classically hourglass shaped. She's demure; I tend to speak my mind. She's British; I'm American. What does it matter? Here we are traveling and laughing together, communicating quite well. It makes us even dearer, our secret world of half-silent sisterhood.

How to teach Anna? I think not only lip reading. I have had practice since Father speaks, having become hard-of-hearing in his teens after an illness. It took me years, though I'm quite adept when talking about common things in common circumstances; I grasp only the gist in less ordinary circumstances with Hearing strangers, or when searching for lips through the jungle of facial hair on some men.

Unlike Father and some of my Deaf friends, I've chosen not to speak aloud, although I've tediously learned how. If you sound like you are deaf in your pronunciation, you risk being treated like you're a lunatic, ignorant, disabled. Especially in modulating a lady-like volume, or a seemly sound to a man, Mother says. Better for the Hearing to know I cannot hear. I can write in my journal for them, use creative signs they understand. We can be clever, collaborate, and I have a sense of humor about our mistakes. Shouldn't we all not take ourselves so seriously?

The train lurches and stops. Emma disembarks to visit a suitor in Philadelphia, our secret little plan. I travel on alone.

A delicious sun-filled day greets me for the final leg of my train trip. Charming towns pass by like Greenwood, Ellendale, Milton, and finally Lewes on the Delaware Bay, the pre-arranged stop my uncle planned for me. He wanted me to see the lovely sailing town with the flavor of my own home town, The Vineyard. He thought the automobile ride and the scenery from Lewes to Rehoboth Beach would charm me.

The train slows, I stand and button up my tan, full-length, silk driving duster to protect my clothes. I don't tie the mesh veil around my sweeping hat just yet, so I can search for Mr. Daniel Spencer who will meet my train. I'm trembling. My usual confidence wanes. What was I thinking?

But allowing Mother to be right is not an option. I lower my window as the train comes to a stop.

I spot a young gentleman on the platform flicking his eyes from a photograph to each passenger. He reaches my gaze, smiles and waves. "Miss Lambert? Miss Grace Lambert? Daniel Spencer." He takes off his hat, exposing shiny locks of thick chestnut hair and looks up at me. We smile, he bows, and shakes my gloved hand through the open window.

I move through the car with my satchel, and step off the train. Still swaying, I try to get my land legs. Daniel takes my bag and turns his head forward to negotiate the crowd. I skitter a few steps ahead to catch what he is saying. He towers over me, making lip reading a stress to my neck, but he's minimally mustachioed, thank goodness. I catch the words *uncle, just arrived from Philadelphia*, and enough to learn that he is the son of my uncle's dear deceased business partner; he's also visiting for the summer. So far I am able to understand the gist; I'm grateful that he speaks slowly, his mouth expressive. His energy is charming, his frame handsome, and his azure eyes don't seem to take notice of my deafness.

The porter, who had followed behind, loads my luggage into Daniel's new Austro-Daimler Prince Henry, and the powerful and elegant car takes us at a frightening speed to the lovely beach town on the Atlantic Ocean.

I arrive in Rehoboth Beach, and find Uncle George, Aunt Julia and several guests, all in a worrisome state. The guests are over-solicitous of me; I'm unaccustomed to being viewed as the unfortunate deaf woman. It causes a clenching in my stomach. I am invited to go into Anna's room to meet her privately.

Her room is darkened, drapes closed; one slice of late sunlight cuts the room in two. I turn on the light. Anna scowls at me, and rearranges her gangly teenage limbs on the chair with no regard for her lovely yellow dress.

Anna, you don't remember me. Cousin Grace, I write in my journal and hand it to her.

She scans the page. No reaction.

The new silence must be frightening for her. I put my hand on her knee.

Anna pushes my journal aside, curls up and casts her eyes down.

Taking my journal back, I write, *you are angry, aren't you?* I receive no answer. I'm angry sometimes, too, I add to the page. I kneel down next to Anna's chair, and put my hand on her cheek. She lowers her eyes again, and presses her lips together tightly to prevent her tears.

I was like you when I was a little girl, too. Deaf my whole life. I have secrets to share, I write. A slight flicker of interest lights Anna's eyes when she reads the word *secrets*—a word a teenage girl can't resist. *I have tricks to show you, how to know what everyone is saying. Did they tell you I'm a teacher?*

Anna rubs her eyes, and takes the journal to write in. *I'm deaf, so now I'll be dumb too, like you, Mommy says.*

I'm stunned at my aunt's ignorance. *I went to school with other Deaf children,* I write. *Some already speak, some learn to talk, some don't. I had Hearing and Deaf friends, published a book on teaching children who are deaf. I play the piano, do you?* I continue to fill the page trying to engage her.

She nods. Her eyes go big with questions, but Anna holds on to her silence.

I write, *Sometimes our angry or scared thoughts inside us get so loud, we can't hear the happy ones, right?*

Anna nods her admission.

My mother taught me to unlace my heart.

"Unlace? That's silly." Anna takes my bait. "What are you angry about? You're so pretty, and you're used to it," she says.

I have no way of knowing if her words sound acceptable to a Hearing person, but I'm pleased she finally speaks. *Want to know what angry voices are in me, Anna?* I write.

She shrugs, feigns disinterest, listens and watches, reading my jottings with suspicious eyes.

I gesture and mime an unlacing of my heart, like releasing a corset and I sigh, and begin writing. *I was betrothed but my fiancé chose another woman; neighbors call me a spinster.*

Anna reads my script. *Why? You're still young and elegant,* Anna instinctively writes, and fingers the gold band on my fountain pen.

I take the journal back and write, *It feels better to tell you my angry thoughts. We'll be special friends. You'll learn to have fun without sounds, I promise you. You can speak if you wish, and see, and touch, and write, and learn to read lips some, feel the vibrations of music, be anything you dream of. And I will teach you and your parents American Sign Language, ASL, so you can talk with other Deaf people.*

I sign, *I love you*, touch my palm to my chest, cross my hands over my heart, then point to Anna. She understands, and a smile fights its way onto her face.

"You truly promise?" Sobbing, she lets me take her into my arms, and we begin.

The weeks press on and May turns into June. Anna and I spend hours in lessons and walking the boardwalk, signing. She is quick to learn and has given up her moodiness. Often we coincidentally run into Daniel, and often not so coincidentally. Anna is very close to him and he helps her to modulate her speech, so solicitous of her, like a brother.

After Daniel's parents perished on one of Uncle George's ships at sea, he'd become the son my uncle never had, and is now heir to the family shipping business, Anna tells me.

Daniel steps in front of us on the boardwalk, juggling three cups. "Ice cream, ladies?" He remembers our favorites, vanilla and strawberry. He seems more than curious about me. I'm threatened by his apparent feelings, and my growing fantasies about this handsome young Hearing man.

He catches me alone late one afternoon in front of the post office. "I don't know how to compliment you without insulting every other woman on earth, but I quite adore your silence," he says.

I focus carefully to read his lips, laugh, trying to avoid an unladylike vocalization.

Mr. Spencer, I intend to tell the world you see all women as chattering nuisances, Dodo birds, I write.

His eyes sparkle and drop a tear, he laughs so hard. "It's just that so much of what's being said these days isn't worth hearing, don't you think?"

I am again grateful that he forms his words so slowly, distinctly, deliberately with lips that seem to want me to understand; and I do. He speaks so much like Father, considerate, and his body participates in the telling.

He's quiet for a moment, pensive. "Since my parents' passing, you are the first to make me laugh." He moves closer. "You're so…" His eyes are speaking now.

I raise my guard, write my tedious speech, and turn it toward him. *Mr. Spencer…* I write.

"*Daniel*, please." He reaches out to stop my pen's motion. Engages my eyes.

I cross out Mr. Spencer. *Daniel, we come from two quite different cultures, won't you concede?*

He leans over my journal and reads it. "Why yes, I suppose, you from that rebellious, liberal Massachusetts culture, me from Philadelphia, a veritable jungle of savages." His grin jumps across, spreads on my own face against my will, and I turn red like an ingénue. He charms me.

Again, I read his lips easily because he graciously slows, tilts his head down to assist me, and I'm so attentive. I squeeze my eyes at him. *I am referring to you being a Hearing person and me, Deaf*, I write. My ink runs dry; I fumble for my spare pen. I imagine a life of scribbling on paper and misunderstanding, missing what his lips have shared. I imagine him standing with his head tilted, shoulders shrugged, trying to understand the nuance of my words, my feelings. So impossible. And, there's Mother…

"As for your hearing or not," he began. I can see by his body language that he is very serious. "I see nothing but a second language, like you speaking French, perhaps without the snobbery; me, some unpolished version of the King's English." He leans his hand against the lamppost. "What if I were to learn to move my own hands so you would understand me?" His hand barely brushes my temple to replace a stray strand of my hair. So intimate, I shouldn't allow it, but I do. "A secret world to live in," he says. "Two silent luh…uh…friends," he stumbles, corrects himself.

I know his lips were forming the word lovers. I swoon.

He goes on. "I'm quite over all the chattering in public places, anyway. And in private, how wonderful to be soundless with you. Forgive me, your face and cleverness alone are worth the journey."

I watch his expressive lips, read his eyes, his smile, the lean of his body. His quick gaze down my summer white cotton blouse and skirt burns me; my temperature rises from his flirtation. I know this is charming and thrilling for now, but there is no destination to this adventure except heartbreak for both of us.

Then he tells me he'll be leaving immediately for Washington, D.C. Some business, maybe life-changing.

I'm wordless, and I work to keep my face emotionless, and come to my senses. *Mr. Spencer, it's getting late, don't you agree?* His disappointment reaches across and clenches my heart. If only, but our futile intercultural fate is certain. I can never live in his world, nor he in mine. For once Mother is right, and he is leaving in the morning. So that's that.

"I'll write. Postcards. Will you write, as well?" He spins his straw hat, drops his head. "My time in Washington is…imperative, vital. Someday, I'll explain."

No need. My words are barely legible.

His lips want to speak, but he turns away, thinks better of it, turns back, and kisses me on the lips boldly in public, engaging my eyes with a message I can't help but hear. I feel him take vital parts of me with his departure—my ability to breathe, think straight. I walk as if my shoes are weighed down by a full bucket of sand. But it's over. I'm relieved that his departure so simply solves my dilemma, but not my heartache, doubly broken in such a short time.

Anna is doing so well. She has the benefit of speech and her father says her words are growing free of deaf awkwardness. That stings me; but I know his comment is innocent. She is learning to be expressive with her Sign Language. I'm amazed at her skill in so few months. Her relieved parents have found a school for the deaf in Washington, D.C. for the fall.

I receive a delightful postcard from Daniel. A sweet surprise. Then another and another, daily. I dutifully return the favor. We turn to letters for privacy as we become more intimate in our exchanges: *Dear Miss Lambert, Dear Grace, My Dear Grace, Darling Grace, My Only One.* I gasp and respond, *Dear Mr. Spencer,* cross it out, *Dear Daniel.*

I find a new hobby, secretly lingering in the heat with the crowd outside the Rehoboth Beach Post Office to await each day's delivery. Pathetic, for a woman of self-possession, but I succumb.

The summer's end is imminent, and I walk from the Post Office empty handed, again and again. No word of his plan to return. I want to go home where I can breathe, begin to accept the loss. Foolish to have let it go this far. I brace myself to extricate the swoon of his presence from my mind. Why does he keep me close with his desk drawer full of postage stamps?

The week before I'm to leave, while dressing, I see his automobile from my window. Thrilled and fearful, I primp in the mirror, press my lilac dress with shaking hands, and rush downstairs.

Curiously, Aunt Julia and Uncle George allow us time alone. I'm propped against the fireplace mantle for support when Daniel enters arguing his case in near flawless American Sign Language. Newly clean-shaven, he makes his lips fully available to me. I nearly slip to the floor. He has been to Gallaudet University, he says—a private tutor, intensive, eight-hour days, nights signing in silent conversation groups, nearly three months—his life-changing work in Washington was...me!

"I intend to dedicate myself to your happiness," Daniel signs.

I'm duly impressed. Quivering, I sign, "No."

We spend hours on the boardwalk arguing the issues. I'm less afraid of losing him now than later, when reality sets in. Too painful.

I can't live in a Hearing world, expatriated from my Deaf culture, I write.

"We'll live in Chilmark; summer here."

I'll surely confuse what your lips are saying, you'll get frustrated, leave me.

He smiles, writes, *Does the sun leave the sky?* then adds, *then speak aloud to me, if I'm unclear.*

No, never! Those aren't sounds you'd want to hear.

His signing vocabulary inadequate, Daniel writes, *You're beyond your sounds, my love. I'm deaf to anything but our loving bond. Your silence, your sounds, awkward or not, no matter, your choice. More likely you'll tire of me.*

Impossible. My tears threaten. I question my sanity; chastise my heart. I write, *Alright then, contingent on my parents' blessings.* Cowardly of me. Consent is customary, not required, but to survive my Chilmark world, Daniel must survive Mother's scrutiny and fixed opinions. I have little hope.

In transit home I coach him. How to hold his body, facial expressions, the silence, so much more than simply using signs or finger spelling. Our hands touch often; I scream for joy in my silence. His sign language is open and expressive. I teach him to ask Father for my hand in marriage.

"Let's practice the kiss again, not sure I have it down." Daniel signs.

Of course, he would have learned the sign for kiss, I think, and I smile, still questioning my wisdom, not my feelings.

We breathe, and enter my parents' home. Daniel's signing hesitations make him simply seem like a nervous suitor.

Fewer words seem manly. I never say he's Hearing; I never say he's Deaf; he's Daniel.

Father consents, delighted with my new Deaf fiancé. Mother takes me aside, her hands flow like a symphonic conductor, beautiful words of congratulations. "Handsome, bright, mannerly, and successful. I've always said my daughter had wisdom," Mother signs so that Daniel cannot see her complimenting hands.

"Did you?" I smile as I sign to Mother. "So I'll not shrivel up after all?"

The telephone rings; our maid is preparing dinner; I instinctively ask Daniel to answer without thinking. Daniel crosses the room and answers. It is Uncle George.

I read Daniel's lips, and he keeps repeating, "Thank you, sir. ...Yes, we're elated. ...Mr. and Mrs. Lambert? ...Yes, so happy, they approve. Yes, we'll summer with you, winters, Grace will teach. I'll work from here with your approval, George."

Mother's face goes ashen. Her signs are deliberate. "So, you purposely tricked me? He's Hearing?"

"No, Mother," I sign. "I let Daniel have a chance to communicate, so you couldn't discriminate. You quite loved him only seconds ago. How quickly the wisdom you just attributed to me for my choice in men escapes me, Mother. The doors of prejudice swing both ways."

"I can't believe it, Charles, he's Hearing!" Mother signs.

"Yes, and he can read your impolite words," Father says, and grins at me.

Daniel signs to bridge our situation. "I love your daughter; I love her silence; I hear her voice without her speaking;

I love how we understand each other. She's beautiful, funny, brilliant. Some things are beyond words, I've learned."

I cross the room on weak legs, and take his flattering hands in mine. Could my chest swell any larger? I find my courage, speak aloud with no fear of sounding awkward, like a lunatic, ignorant, or disabled, "Daniel isn't Hearing, Mother; he is Daniel, and I see Daniel, and he hears me."

And for the first time he truly does.

13. STORM DAMAGE

Photo Courtesy of Rehoboth Beach Historical Society and Museum

The Storm

by Ellen Collins

There is that time before a storm, those hours when the sky is a gentle porcelain blue and the waves lap quietly on the sand, when no one would believe, if you were to tell them, that in twelve hours it would all change so dramatically. That within those twelve hours purple clouds would bruise the sky, the waves would lose all sense of their direction and would pound on the shore, biting into it like an angry mouth. No one would think, much less utter, the word "storm" in those calm hours, when the air is punctuated by the squawk of carefree gulls, their wide wings catching the sun on their feathers. When the horizon is a straight line of the deepest teal, when the breeze feels like velvet.

And who can say when the air changes? It does not happen with drama or decisiveness. It is not as if in one moment you are feeling the soft wind in your hair and in the next your clothes are practically torn off your body. It is not as if in one moment the sky is the pure cerulean of an artist's palette and in the next it roils with dark smudges of indigo and violet and green-gray. The small waves that curl around your ankles do not suddenly rear up and shake their foam like wild horses racing from the north. It is subtle, the coming of a storm.

So that morning, when I was walking barefoot along the beach, carrying my shoes and cotton stockings in my hand, there was no premonition, no warning. The late August air was golden and warm on my back, the waves jaunty as they rolled in and broke on the sand. The hem of my long skirt brushed my leg above my ankles, and I was careful to stay out of reach of the water. High tide was still hours away, and I wandered along the last wrack line. The autograph of the sea, I liked to call it. It always told a story. Clumps of sea cabbage and kelp, fragments of crustacean shells, a broken carapace of a horseshoe crab, gull feathers. Everything came from somewhere, from some being. I often looked at a shell and wondered how far it had traveled, what currents brought it here to this Atlantic shore. I thought of how far I had traveled, not in distance measured in miles but from my life as a wife to my life as a widow. Grief, I was learning, had no clear landmarks, no sense of any destination.

That morning I found a pale gray whelk egg case, like a coiled necklace. There were tangled strands of sea lettuce, broken sand crab legs, shards of scallop shells, and the human relics of a bathing cap, a dented child's pail, a curl of red ribbon. I searched among the detritus and picked out a handful of intact jingle shells, transparent ovals the color of ginger ale. These I would string with fishing line to hang with the hundreds of others I already had crisscrossing my kitchen window. Down by the water, a dozen sandpipers did their staccato dance in the lace of the ebb and flow of the waves. A fat gray gull perched like a sentry on a wooden piling, and a group of five pelicans flew by, their wings beating up and down with the precision of water ballet. It was a glorious morning to be alive.

Shells held carefully in my hand, I made my way across the sand and up the stairs to the boardwalk. The boards under my feet had been smoothed by thousands of other feet, although this early in the morning there were only a few others out and about. A couple of boys, about nine years old, rode their bikes, standing up on the pedals to catch the breeze in their hair. Several older women, wearing wide-brimmed hats, walked purposefully, their steps measured and even, getting exercise so they could justify sitting under an umbrella on the sand all day. A young couple sat on a green bench, and he gently rocked a wicker pram to quiet their baby back to sleep.

Seeing a couple like that never failed to make me catch my breath, caught in memory. How many benches had James and I sat on? How many times had I felt his hand on my shoulder that way? Since his death the previous autumn, I always felt like I walked around acutely aware of who was not with me. That the small of my back, where he always touched me when we walked together, was a space acutely tuned to absence. It almost hurt. When, I wondered, would my back return to just being a back, with no recollection of that ghost impression?

I always loved walking here before the crowds came, when the air had that fresh salt tang. As I passed by the two-story houses with their wide porches, the sun bright on the windows, I thought how lucky the families were who lived there, who could awaken each morning to the watercolor wash of sunrise over the horizon. I thought how lucky they were to go to sleep each night to the lullaby song of the waves as the tides rolled in and out. I could only afford a small house a few miles inland, but I tried to start each day walking on the shore. The ocean sounded like breathing to me, and I would close my eyes and inhale (I breathe in calm) and let the air out slowly (I breathe out sorrow). With time, I hoped, I could exhale all the sorrow that now filled me, not only in my lungs and heart but all the way to my toes, the tips of my ears.

Farther along, I stopped at a café and sat at one of the small round tables. I ordered tea and a cranberry muffin, and while the tea cooled I buckled my shoes in preparation for going home. I hated to leave. Home was a one-bedroom bungalow with the sofa, the dining table, and the bookcases I had had in New York. Home was the dishes I had eaten on for twenty years, the secretary desk with the glass-fronted shelves and the stained inkwell. Home was my dresses and my rolling pin and my grandmother's crocheted afghan. But home felt empty and was really just a house, walls that surrounded my possessions. I doubted I would ever say the word "home" and hear echoes of words like welcome, comfort, connection. I had lost all sense of what home really meant when James died in October.

So I would have stayed there all day if I could have, watching the sunbathers come with umbrellas, blankets, picnic hampers. I would have watched the day fill up with the color of voices, the song of children laughing and gulls screeching. I would have looked over at those initials carved in the railing and daydreamed about all the lovers who had walked here, who had held hands and run across the sand, who had kissed in the shadows outside the pools of moon-light. And I would know that after the crowds departed, when the copper sun dropped into the western bay, the place would belong to me again. For now, though, the own-er of the bookshop where I worked expected me to unlock the door at ten o'clock. As I headed away from the board-walk, I thought that perhaps I would return that evening for a picnic supper, just me and the gulls.

In truth, I could happily have spent whole days just watching the ocean, the dimples on the water marking schools of fish, the acrobatics of the dolphins, the slow grace of osprey in flight from the water to their high nests. I had moved to the beach seeking healing. We had lived in New York all of our married life, but after his death I had felt jarred by the jangle of city life. Traffic, tall buildings, the clatter of horse-drawn carriages, the cries of sidewalk vendors. After the startling short weeks of his illness when I sat by his side in the darkened bedroom, I craved open spaces. I wanted to pare everything down to the basics of land and sea and sky. I wanted people in my life, yes, but I also wanted the solitude of an empty stretch of sand or the quiet of a salt marsh. I wanted to stand at night under an endless display of firefly stars where the only music would be a lonely owl. That was the music I heard in my own heart.

I was busy all morning at the bookstore, sorting and pricing books in the stockroom. And yes, I read a chapter or two. How could I be expected to handle all those books and not read any of them? So it wasn't until around one, when I went into the front of the store to retrieve my lunch from under the counter, that I knew there was a storm brewing. Ruth, the other clerk, and I stood at the door and looked out at the street, where scraps of paper swirled like fallen leaves, and it looked like it was much later than early afternoon. The few people who were on the street seemed intent on getting somewhere, unlike the usual parade of window shoppers. The sky had darkened to an ominous charcoal.

His illness had started in August with an innocent cough. "Nothing to worry about," he had assured me, but the dry hacking increased, until he was up half the night sitting in a chair in the living room.

I suggested he check in with his doctor. "You have to get a good night's sleep. Maybe he can give you some cough medicine."

"It's just an allergy. I'm fine. Really, I think it's getting better."

But it wasn't, and the dry cough deepened until I could hear it rumble in his chest.

It was a golden early September day when he came into the kitchen where I was rolling out a piecrust and leaned against the door. He was holding his hand to his chest.

"I think there might be something wrong. Maybe it's time for the doctor." He was pale, and there was a shine of perspiration on his forehead. His green eyes were unnaturally bright. A shaft of cold sunlight cut across the counter like a knife.

Pneumonia works fast, and nothing made it better. Not the compresses, not the tincture of potassium iodide, not the low doses of digitalis. Within a month James was dead.

As I watched the darkening skies from the shop door, I wondered what had happened to the gentle morning air. Had it only been five hours before that I had sat drinking tea on the boardwalk, lulled by the murmur of the surf? I thought about the swiftness of a storm, like the swiftness of illness. Last fall we had heard about the ravages of pneumonia, but it always happened to someone else, not to a healthy man in his early fifties. As I watched the street, the first raindrops fell, fat splats of water on the sidewalk. Then the drops changed to pelting, and gusts of rain slapped the screen so that I had to push the heavy outside door closed. Ceiling lights flickered.

"We should close up," Ruth said. "No one's going to come in today." I realized then that I had not heard the voices of customers for several hours. We could see across the street that awnings had been rolled up, shades drawn. We clicked off the lights and turned the OPEN sign around.

Throughout the afternoon the wind showed no signs of slowing down. No mercy for the beach town with its pastel houses and weathered shingled roofs. No mercy for the pilings that held up the wide planks of the boardwalk, or for the flagpoles and the storefront awnings. The wind tore off shutters and flattened dunes. It uprooted slender trees and trampled the geraniums and lobelia in the town square, flung porch furniture like toys and plucked mailboxes up by their stalks.

The storm continued to rage throughout the evening. Rain smacked the windows of my cottage, wind screamed around the chimney. The pines in my yard bent and bounced. I lived far enough inland to be safe from flooding, but I kept thinking about the houses I had looked at that morning, houses that hugged the shore. What would it be like to be so close to the ocean during this storm? I imagined most of the people who lived there had evacuated farther inland. I passed the evening in candlelight, not knowing what was happening beyond the perimeter of my home. Instead of the beach picnic I had planned, I ate a cheese sandwich on my sofa, with the windows rattling in their frames and rain beating insistently on the roof.

As much as I loved the drama of a storm, it was at times like this that I missed James the most. If he had been here, we would have sat together watching the frenzy of lightning, counting the seconds between the flash and the crack of thunder. If a shutter blew off, how would I replace it? If a tree crashed on the roof, who would help me figure out what to do? Sitting in the darkness listening to the furious storm, I was afraid. I was lonely. I did not feel at all like the capable woman who was recreating her broken life. I wanted James to hold me and tell me we would be all right.

Sometime in the night, while I slept in fitful dreams, the storm moved on. When I woke up the house was strangely quiet, as if it were afraid to breathe. My yard was littered with fallen branches, the bird feeder had toppled over into the hydrangea bushes, and I saw one of my porch chairs in the street. Puddles of rainwater in the street glistened faintly in the thin beams of the sun that had begun to edge out from behind the shredding clouds.

By midmorning the clouds had drifted away and the sky was washed clean and blue. I remembered the day after James's funeral. It had been a clear day like this, and there was a stillness I had never experienced, like everything had stopped. I had moved slowly through the house, picking up random objects—an ashtray, a letter opener, his comb. I touched things and put them down. I checked the grandfather clock in the front hall to see if the pendulum was still swinging; sure that time must have halted and left me in empty rooms, unable to move either forward or back. I could not imagine ever being hungry again, or mopping the floor, or putting the slipcovers on the couches when the season changed.

With the sun out, I decided to go investigate, to find people to talk with, to see if the bookstore still had windows intact. I walked through the quiet streets, saw a few other curious pedestrians, bicyclists slowly navigating through intersections, the occasional Model T chugging along, veering around tree limbs and other debris. At the center of town most of the shops were still closed, so I walked toward the ocean, thinking of the shells the storm had probably left in its wake on the beach. I would walk along the boardwalk to my favorite spot near the jetty and see what I could collect. Not just the small jingle shells of yesterday, but maybe a conch shell, some driftwood, even a shard or two of sea glass.

Except there was no boardwalk.

Where it had been was now a rubble of broken planks of wood. Wood splintered and split, cracked and soaking wet. It was like a giant pile of pick-up sticks, flung by a careless hand. A light pink house I had seen yesterday had lost its porch and most of its roof. It had collapsed into itself. Many of the other houses that fronted the ocean lay in ruins as well, walls gaping open to reveal living rooms filled with ceiling beams, upturned chairs and tables. Porch stairs were twisted off and lay in the rubble of rocks and sand. The dunes that had curved up from the earth, waving with green and amber oat grass, had been chewed out and sheared off into steep cliffs. In some places, there were not even cliffs, but flat sand that stretched from the berm and under the pilings beneath the lopsided houses.

Yesterday I had found the story of the ocean at the wrack line. Today the wrack line was a somber narration of the storm and the people who had felt its brute force. As I picked my way through broken boards, I saw a story that had come to an abrupt conclusion, and I saw the people who had been in the story. In the chipped terra cotta pot with plant roots hanging from it like disheveled hair, I saw the woman who loved flowers and had lined her porch with pots of bright blooms. In the deflated red and blue rubber ball and the painted metal shovel poking through a heap of wood, I saw the children who played on the beach, running in and out of the waves. In a broken cup, in a wrought iron table leg, I saw the people who sat outside the cafe. In the ripped sign ("Ice cream cones—1 penny") and the water-logged menus, I saw the shopkeepers. In the bent chairs and the mattress still covered with its white sheet, I saw the homeowners. In every creosote-soaked broken board, every metal lamp covering, every shard of glass, every scrap of awning, I saw and heard the voices that had rung in the late summer air.

It had been like that in our house the day after the funeral. James was everywhere. He was in his typewriter with a sheet of paper in the roller, the fresh stack of paper next to it on the desk. He was in the 1904 World's Fair mug with the black drawing of the Cascade Gardens. He was in his starched shirts hanging in his closet, in the metal tin of oxblood shoe polish. He lingered in the chair where he sat to read the newspaper, in his sock drawer, in the keys and cufflinks on top of his dresser. He was in the stack of old Life magazines he refused to throw away. Everywhere I looked that day, I saw him, and it even seemed that I could hear his laugh. There was hardly anything I could touch that did not bring him to me, and yet he was not there.

The storm had done more than destroy a boardwalk and some houses. It had done more than uproot trees and flatten the dunes. It had taken away early morning walks on those wide planks. It had washed away strolling along trying to eat the chocolate ice cream before it melted down the side of the cone. It had stilled the conversations and confidences of midnight stargazers who leaned on the railings watching the black ocean swells. It had, in a few hours, eroded a way of life.

James's death had changed everything too. I stumbled when I started to say, "We…" I didn't know which side of the bed to sleep on. His death took away the second table setting at dinner, and milk soured before I could drink it all. I was living a life based on memory, and I wasn't sure if it would be possible to rebuild anything else. I was afraid that the memories would start to fade, and I would be left with nothing. When I left the city for a new life in this beach town, I had brought things with the deepest memory reservoirs: his typewriter, his watch, his set of the complete works of Shakespeare, his leaky fountain pen. I would have given anything to be able to scold him again for carrying that pen in his jacket pocket.

The storm had underscored the hard reality that nature is both spellbinding and destructive, and there is a thin line between those two identities. How long would it be before the shops opened and the sweet tang of caramel corn permeated the air, before the bright umbrellas dotted the beach, before families gathered at twilight on those wide porches facing the sea, before sand and wind could work together to build up the dunes again? How long would it be before I would wake up not puzzled that his pillow was cool and unwrinkled?

Above me the sky was a benevolent blue. Gulls circled in the air or bobbed lazily on the rolling waves. The sun touched the top of my head, and the breeze carried its usual salt scent. I looked at the wide beach where I had thought I might find treasures—that conch, the odd-shaped driftwood, the jade sea glass. There was only the wide swath of sand, dotted here and there with a solitary plank or sometimes whole intact sections of the boardwalk. Whatever the wild tides had brought in, the wilder wind had swept away. I leaned over and picked up a handful of sand and let it sift down through my fingers. It had only been twenty-four hours. How many more before this storm would be a distant memory and the bright, beautiful story of the beach could begin again?

14. WOMEN IN BATHING SUITS

Photo Courtesy of Rehoboth Beach Historical Society and Museum

Postcard from Rehoboth Beach 1897

by Sherri Wright

Dear Cousin Caroline,
Granny expects us to stroll like ladies
with long skirts and parasols to
protect ourselves
she makes us promise
to come home before dark

When you visit we'll show you
how we slip
into the bathhouse
under the boardwalk   don
our (scanty) dresses and wade in
up to our waists we laugh
at the men who act like boys rolling
and splashing in the surf but when
they yell for us to dive right in

we scurry back to the bathhouse
dry our salty bodies
lace up corsets and high top
shoes and strut (like ladies)
down the boardwalk
and into Granny's front porch
before sun sets on the Rehoboth sky

Your loving cousins
Ruby and Violet

Captured

by Linda Federman

As the brig-sloop De Braak escorted a merchant flotilla sailing from England through the Azores on its way to Virginia in February of 1798, a curtain of fog descended and her navigator lost sight of the other ships. Sailing along alone, she came upon us, The Don Francisco Xavier. Beads of nervous sweat dripped from my mustache, and my guts knotted as Captain James Drew and his men swarmed our decks, seizing the opportunity to capture our ship, our cargo of copper bars and cocoa, and all of the men aboard. Our caramel-skinned sailors, muscular and wind-blown, started diving off the bow, free-falling toward the vast and endless ocean. Better to be swallowed by the open mouth of the sea than be imprisoned—or worse—on an unfamiliar continent. "Si tengo que morir al menos moriré libre"—"If I have to die, at least I'll die free"—they shouted as they jumped. But only a few made it over before the invaders snatched those of us who were still within their reach.

In the end a dozen of us—shaken, terrified, and mourning our lost brothers—were taken aboard the De Braak and became unwilling guests on passage to North America.

The De Braak and her quarry arrived at last in Delaware Bay on May 25, 1798 and put in at Cape Henlopen to board a fresh pilot. The sky was heavenly blue. A handful of gossamer-wing clouds drifted along like languid angels. We loaded provisions as the new pilot received reports from the crew that had been aboard. Accounts of food stores, ammunition, provisions, oil for lamps, candles. Condition updates on the masts and sails and riggings. The tools and water stores tallied and replenished. We heaved wooden barrels, bolted together with iron rivets, into the hold. Under the fierce glare of our captors, we counted and stacked, polished brass and replaced lines, and shooed rats out of the rafters. Not one of us dared step out of line, not one attempted a clandestine sip of water. To do so would result in the lash of a whip or the blow of a gun stock to the side of the head.

Looking back now I wonder why those clouds brought to mind angels. Had I been paying more attention might I not have thought it a premonition? Might I have thought to relish the fair wind, to turn my face to the gentle stroke of the sun? If I'd known it would be my final hours in that body, would I have stopped to savor the last flavors of life?

Distracted by our labors, no one noticed that the clouds had started to thicken, clumping together and darkening as the delicate spring breeze stiffened and turned. It swung in from the east like a cold fist, and soon was whistling through the riggings, whipping the sails and our shirt tails, drying our sweat to a cold, salty film prickled by gooseflesh.

The wind pounded the side of the hull, the wood creaking and groaning in protest. The De Braak pitched and tossed as the waves rose and tilted the 340-ton ship as easily as a toy in a rain barrel. She listed sharply, and I fell and slid across the deck, picking up splinters and slamming against the rails before being tipped into the water like tea leaves from a drained cup. The ocean slapped my face as I broke the surface, then it pulled me under. Chunks of broken wood and iron swirled about and pelted me. I could taste my own blood in my mouth mixing with the salt. The heft and velocity of the sinking ship gave birth to its own universe, creating a force that pulled everything with it even as it broke itself to bits. I tumbled over and around. Everything tumbling until there was no up or down, no possibility of swimming up—up to air, up to my life. I tried to grab a passing rope that seemed like it was floating towards the surface, but in fact might have been sinking in the gravitational field of the ship.

As I grasped for it I felt a tiny surge of hope—hope that this slender cord would be my salvation. That I could grab its knotted end and together we would save me. Then a piece of jagged wood struck my face. My teeth exploded and swam around inside my mouth.

That's the moment I gave up and let go. I stopped holding my breath and inhaled the water deeply. It filled my lungs, and for a moment I was a baby in the womb once again, hovering on the cataclysmic edge of evolution when fish are made human. Only this time in reverse.

As I filled with seawater I thought about my mother, who died bringing me into that life. Would I see her again? I thought about my father, an angry and usually drunk man from whom I ran to join the Spanish sailors.

And I thought about love. Aside from the vigorous groping of village girls and frantic sweaty encounters with women of low morals in ports all over Europe and the Caribbean, I had never really been in love. And now there would be no chance for that to ever happen.

I surrendered to the swaddling comfort of the water. I stopped flailing and grasping about. I welcomed all that brine into every cell. And I drifted off into what seemed like a deep sleep after a night of heavy drinking.

Longing to feel love was the last thing I remember about life in the body of a man.

That sudden storm had swept through the harbor on the wings of demons, taking the well-seasoned captain and his crew by surprise, capsizing his ship and drowning her crew of forty as well as a dozen Spanish prisoners. And me.

I remember what that life felt like, the one in which I walked in a man's body. But memory now is different. I remember the sensations, but only weakly, like distant foghorns. I remember it as if it happened to someone else, and I had only heard the tales; a memory of someone else's memory. And in a way, this is indeed the case.

I remember how as a young boy I first fell in love with the sea when I went to the docks and heard the music of boatmen's bells, smelled the shimmering fish they spilled into barrels, and saw the wild-eyed women who welcomed them home. I remember dimly what it was like to feel leather boots brushing against shins; lips cracked from too much sun and too little fresh water; the comfort of a lumpy mattress and scratchy blanket against aching muscles and sunburned shoulders at the end of a day at sea. And I remember lying in that bunk wishing there would be one of those women pining for me to come home.

I find myself now, or a version of myself, wandering the Delaware peninsula where yet another sea had claimed the De Braak, leaving me captive forever on the coast to which

I was dragged. Sometimes I soar above the shore, other times I shuffle along the tideline. I can't feel the sand between my toes, but if I reach and grasp at it, at the echo of that sensation, I can remember what it once felt like. The shift of it beneath every step, the touch of it at once soft and gritty. And that deep ache when one dares to think how the miniscule grains were once solid rock from a faraway place and time.

I watch the seasons turn, and yet time is not a linear parade of days like it was in the body. It turns and dips and loops back on itself and lurches forward. It's like the shipwreck in which I drowned, bits and pieces floating and swirling with no point of reference for up or down, forward or back. An endless parade of changing fashions, changing dialects, buildings and streets erected and torn down.

I watch the people as they come and go. Bundled in coats and cloaks and hats and gloves and form-hugging stretch pants, a sparse few brave the shore in colder months. In some eras they wear modest swimsuits down to their ankles in the summer despite the heat; in others they wear next to nothing.

Hemlines go up and down and hairstyles go in and out of favor, but the love dance of humanity remains constant. Teenagers tease and flirt and laugh too loudly at each other's antics. Lovers hold hands or glare at each other during quarrels that will quickly be forgiven with a kiss. Mates meld into families and the children grow to have children of their own. Older people with weathered faces and gray hair stare at the ocean and mourn loves that they lost.

I myself fall in love over and over. Or in desire. Or whatever the sensation might be that makes me wish I were in a man's body again. To reach out and touch the flesh of one of those glistening women, glowing from the sun and youth and perspiration. In some eras they smell like mildewed wool, in others they smell like coconuts or lavender.

When that desire is its strongest—when it rages inside like a fever, when I long so much to know that dizzying feeling, the kind that makes the heart swell to bursting—I can make myself seen. The kind of longing that sends artists mad, sends poets to jump off bridges, sends warriors across continents for the sake of it. Through the sheer force of that yearning I can make myself seen. I cannot touch nor feel, I cannot make a noise or move an object, but I look down on occasion and see feet, shins, hands. I can project myself into the clothes of the day, but always my face looks as it did when I was in the body. Wavy black hair above a high forehead, wide flat nose, irises so dark they are indistinguishable from the pupils, a narrow chin. Skin color so much paler than my Spanish parents that my father often questioned my legitimacy.

It only happens for a moment or two, but when it does I get as close to the beach people as I can. I have been scratched into their etchings and woodcuts. I have been sketched onto their onion skins and rough yellow pads with charcoals and chalks. I have been painted onto their canvasses. I have been popped into pictures from the earliest photographs created with giant flashes of light and a bit of smoke, to the fantastic magic of cell phones and holograms.

Each time I wonder about them. I wonder who they are, where they go when they leave the labor of fishing; the lazy laying about on the sand eating sandwiches and reading novels; the surfing; the kite-flying and Frisbee tossing; the bird watching and the bonfires. I hope they do not go home alone; I'd rather imagine them in cozy houses, living in the crooked elbow of love.

I think about the people who have captured my image and wonder if they think about me too. Do they imagine who I might be, conjure a life for me—or do they just shrug and dismiss me as a stranger who wandered out of the frame of that moment as inconsequentially as I had wandered in? They'll never know the effort, the will, the longing that had to be harnessed to render myself visible, to hold myself close enough to them to feel the whisper of their breath near my cheek.

I think of them back home hanging those paintings, putting those photos into albums with scrolly cursive captions, framing those sketches to set by the bedside. There I am in the background—behind the gulls or the lifeguard chairs or the umbrellas lined up like a semaphore message; behind grandma and grandpa holding hands, the wind whipping their hair into froth. Or behind two lovely sisters in baggy dark bathing suits that conceal the curves and contours of their bodies, who made my heart ache with their broad smiles, squinting hard against the sun. There I am radiating light from my summer white shirt and pants; radiating a yearning so great I can make myself visible for a moment, as I pass close enough to smell the ocean on their skin.

It is a relief to me to move through other seasons. When the beach grass casts longer shadows across the sand, and the visitors have gone, I can soar and dive alone along the coastline, free from my sad longing. I watch the populations of terns and gulls swell and shrink; the dolphins move closer and then further away from the shore. I watch the mullet shoot out of the water like tossed daggers, sparkling for a moment in a beautiful suicide dance before being plucked out of the air by a diving pelican. The crabs scuttle across the cool sand at night and burrow back under it to escape the blazing sun. The tides go in and out, endlessly, in total velvet darkness or under the smiling moon.

Legends tell of a Sea Witch, a mother-demon who protects the remains of the De Braak by conjuring violent weather to thwart anyone who attempts to salvage the ship and claim her mythological treasure. There is no truth to that rumor, although it is a romantic notion. I sometimes would like it to be true. I'd like to think that I am not the only lonely spirit on this stretch of beach, not the only soul who pines through eternity for love.

Rehoboth Beach 1977

by Irene Fick

We were sun worshippers, grilling
baby-oiled flesh in lace bikinis all day long,
our bellies taut, thighs not yet puckered.
We lolled on rubber rafts, cradled and sipped
rum potions, topped with oranges
and tiny umbrellas. We giggled about Jaws,
made low rumbling sounds,
as if to dare any menace, land or sea,
to disturb our budding power. Later,
we emerged from tumultuous waters, strolled
to big blankets tucked into the gritty sand,
and we lit more cigarettes, downed more rum,
maneuvered our bodies to seize the final rays
of the afternoon. How safe we felt
under the sun's divine embrace, its soft
and tender halo. We were goddesses
and nothing, nothing, could ever hurt us.

CONTRIBUTORS

Terri Clifton resides on a historic farm on the edge of the Delaware Bay near Prime Hook Beach. Her nonfiction, *A Random Soldier*, was released in 2007. In 2013 she was awarded a fellowship for an emerging artist in fiction/literature by the Delaware Division of the Arts. Her short stories have been included in several anthologies, and she recently had her first poem selected for publication. She is also an accomplished photographer, and it was this interest that led to the perspective of the story around the making of the photograph. As the director of a non-profit, Terri speaks on the healing power of art and literacy. She also enjoys travel with her husband, an internationally known wildlife artist.

Ellen Collins is a writer, teacher, and artist who divides her time between Bethany Beach, Delaware and Vienna, Virginia. She taught in Fairfax County Public Schools for twenty-five years and now spends as much time as possible gleaning inspiration from nature. Her work has appeared in *No Place Like Here; The Beach House; Referential;* and *Bellevue Literary Review.* She is the author of a book of poetry, *The Memory Thief,* and co-author with Ginny Daly of *The Guest Book.*

Anne Colwell, a poet and fiction writer, is an Associate Professor of English and Creative Writing at the University of Delaware. She has published two books of poems, *Believing Their Shadows* (Word Poems 2010) and *Mother's Maiden Name* (Word Poems 2013) as well as a book about Elizabeth Bishop (*Inscrutable Houses*, University of Alabama). She received the Established Artist in Fiction Fellowship and the

Established Artist in Poetry Fellowship from the Delaware Division of the Arts, as well as the Mid-Atlantic Arts Fellowship at the Virginia Center for the Creative Arts and three Work-Study Fellowships to the Bread Loaf Writers Conference. Her work has appeared or is forthcoming in journals, including: *Valparaiso Review; Birmingham Arts Journal; r.kv.r.y; Southern Poetry Review; Gargoyle; Prime Number; Carve;* and *Octavo.* She is the poetry editor of *The Delmarva Review.*

Gail Braune Comorat's poetry has appeared in *Gargoyle; Grist;* and *The Widows' Handbook.* She is the author of a poetry chapbook, *Phases of the Moon* (Finishing Line Press). Her short story, "The Hill Girls," is fictionalized from tales she heard from her three great-aunts about their early days in north Wilmington. Gail resides in Lewes, Delaware and is currently working on her first novel.

Linda Federman's writing career began on staff at TDC: The Magazine of The Discovery Channel. In the time since, her freelance restaurant reviews and lifestyle stories have appeared in *The Washington Post; The Washington Times;* and numerous other newspapers and magazines. She served as Managing Editor of special sections for a chain of northern Virginia weeklies, and as a ghost writer on several books and manuscripts. At various times during her two sons' growing-up years, Linda wrote and edited; ran an editorial services and PR company; owned a floral design school; and drove a day camp bus. She and her husband of thirty years are close to realizing their life-long dream of moving to the beach

"888"

full-time, where she plans to "photo bomb" vacationers for many summers to come.

Irene Fick's first collection of poetry, *The Stories We Tell*, was published in 2014 by The Broadkill Press and received first place awards from the National Federation of Press Women (NFPW) and the Delaware Press Association (DPA). Irene's poetry has been published in such journals as *Poet Lore; Gargoyle; The Broadkill Review; Philadelphia Stories; Adanna Literary Journal;* and *Delaware Beach Life.* Her poetry has been nominated for a Pushcart Prize. In 2016, Irene's poem, "Asunder," received the first place award from DPA, and second place from NFPW. A former journalist, Irene worked for newspapers and magazines in Chicago, Tampa, San Francisco and Philadelphia. She directed community affairs for a major medical center in Philadelphia and a global pharmaceutical company in Wilmington, Delaware. Irene lives in Lewes and is active in the Rehoboth Beach Writers Guild and Coastal Writers.

Jessica Gordon, a resident of Lewes, Delaware, is a free-lance writer and founder of Conjure Communications, specializing in nonprofit and small business communications. A frequent contributor to *Delaware Beach Life* magazine, Jess' work has also appeared in *The News Journal; Delaware Today* magazine; and *Delaware State News.* Her work has twice been recognized by the Delaware Press Association. A New York native, Jess grew up on the Hudson River and took vacations to the Atlantic each summer. Her inspiration for "The Ocean Virgins" came from the common experience of enjoying the beach with friends, which transcends time and place.

Gary Hanna lives with his wife, the artist Anne Hanna, on Vines Creek estuary at the end of Indian River Bay near Dagsboro, Delaware. He has received five Individual Artist Awards and two Fellowships from the Delaware Division of the Arts and a Residency Fellowship to the Virginia Center for the Creative Arts. He has published two chapbooks, *The Homestead Poems* and *Sediment and Other Poems*, and many poems in literary journals and anthologies across the country. He likes to write ekphrastic poems and loves shipwrecks.

Crystal Heidel lives in Milton, Delaware. She's previously published a murder mystery, *Still Life in Blood*, that features the Delaware State Police and takes place in Rehoboth and Lewes. *Still Life in Blood* won First Place in both the Delaware Press Association's Communications Contest, and the National Federation of Press Women's Communication Contest in 2014. She's also recently published a collection of poetry, *Landslide*, that tells of bittersweet love and loss. In addition to her writing career, she is the Manager and Lead Graphic Designer at Logo Motive Custom Apparel in Rehoboth, and also does freelance design, including book covers. Her fascination and obsession with history, witchcraft, and old ships was heightened when she saw the *Falmouth* Wreck image on the RBWG website. Instantly drawn into the 19th century lore of ruined ships and the legend of the Bad Weather Witch, she knew she was able to tie a story that had been brewing in the back of her mind to the beautiful, but doomed *Falmouth*.

Bill Hicks's work has appeared in many elementary class-rooms in three states, spanning his thirty-year teaching career, but "The Wreck" is his first published piece. Bill's love of the sea and history was his inspiration to write this short story based on the wreck of the *Falmouth* on Hallow-een Night, 1899. Bill's family has owned a beach house in Lewes since 1963, and he grew up spending summers there. Two years after retiring he and his wife, Jill, a published author in her own right, moved permanently to Lewes to be near the beach they so love. Bill can now be found volun-teering with the Lewes Historical Society, writing Flash Fiction pieces for the Rehoboth Beach Writers Guild's "Art in the AM," or messing about the Bay on his boat.

Wendy Elizabeth Ingersoll is a retired piano teacher and native Delawarean residing outside Newark. Publications include her book *Grace Only Follows*, which won the National Federation of Press Women Contest; two chapbooks; po-ems in *Poetry East; Naugatuck River Review; Connecticut River Review; Cahoodaloodaling; Passager; Gargoyle; Main Street Rag; Mojave River Review; Worcester Review; Hartskill Review; Broadkill Review;* and the anthology *On the Mason-Dixon Line* (Universi-ty of Delaware). Her poems have been awarded first place in contests sponsored by Rehoboth Beach Writers Guild, Milton Poetry Festival, and Delaware Literary Connection. She has five lovely grandchildren and also enjoys serving as reader for *The Delmarva Review*. As inspiration for her poem,

Wendy did actually see a sonar of an ancient sunken ship, though on a tour boat ride on the Chester River rather than Rehoboth Bay. The tour boat captain told of a news reporter mistaking what she'd heard, and the rest of the story continued inside Wendy's head.

Shelley Kahn is employed in federal service as a civil rights attorney. She lives most of the time in the suburbs of Washington, D.C., but her heart is pulled in the direction of the Delaware coast. One of her many passions in life has been to write poetry about everything she has observed in nature, in people and animals. Her poems have been featured in various publications, such as *White Space; Melancholy Hyperbole; The Broadkill Review; Dove Tales Anthology; Moon Magazine; The Path; From the Depths* and *Haunted Water's Press*. She is currently a member of the Rehoboth Beach Writers Guild.

James Keegan's work has appeared in *The Southern Poetry Review; Poet Lore; The Gettysburg Review; Prime Number; Delaware Beach Life;* and *The Best Small Fictions of 2015*. He has a chapbook of poems, *Of Fathers and Sons*, which won the inaugural Dogfish Head Poetry Prize, and he is the featured poet in the current issue of *The Delmarva Review*. His fictional letter from the battlefields of World War I was inspired by his dual interest in that war and in letters as a genre of writing. James is a professional actor who has performed for the last decade as a member of the resident acting company at The American Shakespeare Center. He is also an associate professor of English and Theater for the University of

Delaware in Georgetown. He and his wife, Anne Colwell, live in Milton.

Jack Mackey splits his time between Rehoboth Beach and Washington, D.C. He is a former Beltway bandit and consultant.

Kathleen L. Martens is a resident of Rehoboth Beach and active member of the Rehoboth Beach Writers Guild. Publications include: the award-winning memoir of Margaret Zhao, *Really Enough, a True Story of Tyranny, Courage and Comedy*; short stories: "Molting," 2015 Judge's Choice Award; and "Flight of the Songbird," 2016 First Place winner, Cat and Mouse Press Beach Reads anthologies, and first place winner 2017 Delaware Press Association Communications Awards for a single short story. During her tenure with professional children's theatre, Imagination Stage, Kathleen worked to support the Deaf Access theatre program which inspired her to write, "Hearing is Believing." Her great-grandfather, James Henry King, worked for the Pennsylvania Railroad for fifty-two years, and drove a train that carried the President of the United States. The article from a New York newspaper containing his charming quote from the story, "The Time of His Life," was found while searching her family genealogy.

Alice Morris, resident of Lewes, Delaware since 1986, comes to writing with a background in art; she was published in a West Virginia textbook and *The New York Art Review*. Her poetry appears in *The Broadkill Review; Delaware*

Beach Life; Silver Birch Press; The Avocet; The Weekly Avocet; Rat's Ass Review; and the chapbook *The White Space.* Poetry is also included or forthcoming in themed collections and anthologies, most recently, *Bared: Contemporary Poetry* and *Art on Bras and Breasts.* Her poem, "Under the Wide Open Sky," speaks to the strict rules of the Victorian era.

Rita Nelson has just published her first book, *Always Kristen*, a memoir about her transgender daughter, and is working on her first novel, *Abby*, about domestic abuse. When she saw the 1916 photograph of three young women and a man, it sparked her genealogical imagination about the linkage, lineage, and history of these young people. She has had articles published in *Offshore Magazine; The Seminary Catalog; The AMBO;* and *The Delaware Communion.* While living in Florida in the early 1990's, Rita wrote a column on condominium living for the *Siesta Key Pelican Press* and today continues blogging for her townhome development, and her personal blog, *Wordsfromthecrone.com.* She is also a regular reader at RBWG's Night of Songs and Stories. Rita is an Episcopal Priest who has served churches in Florida and Delaware. She is currently retired and enjoys reading, writing, genealogy, and traveling. She lives in Millsboro, Delaware with her husband, Ralph Peters, daughter Kristen, and AKC Grand Champion Maltese, Loki.

Mary Pauer, twice recipient of a literary fellowship award from the Delaware Division of the Arts, author of the collections *Big Haired Women* and *Traveling Moons,* has published in *Southern Women's Review, The Delmarva Review, The Foxchase*

Review, among other literary journals. She is a speaker and scholar for Delaware Humanities Forum and freelances as a developmental editor for private clients. Recently she adopted a Quarter Horse seized in a case of abuse and neglect. He joins the other animals on the farm who secretly write speculative fiction after lights out.

Russell Reece has had stories and poems published in numerous journals and anthologies including *Delaware Beach Life; The Broadkill Review; The Boardwalk;* and *The Delmarva Quarterly.* In 2007 Russ retired from his position of Vice President and CIO at Playtex Products. Since then he has received several writing awards including fellowships from the Delaware Division of the Arts and the Virginia Center for the Creative Arts. Russ is a native Delawarean who lives near Bethel, Delaware along the beautiful Broad Creek.

Sharon Sheppard's poems have appeared in *South Dakota Magazine,* and she has self-published four poetry books: *All We Ever Wanted; As If It Were Visible; To the Borders of Light;* and *A Single Grain of Sand.* She worked for thirty-seven years in the paper industry, and is now happily retired near kids and grandkids. Sharon writes poetry to process and preserve life's experiences, and enjoys sharing her work with others. Formerly of Isanti, Minnesota, she now lives in Magnolia, Delaware.

Nancy Powichroski Sherman has been a teacher for over forty-two years, but a writer since she was old enough to sit at her bedroom window and imagine. Her short stories have been published in *Delaware Beach Life; Fox Chase Review; Referential; The Beach House* anthology; and her own collection of stories, *Sandy Shorts*, which received national first place honors from the National Federation of Press Women. Upon seeing the photograph of a family sitting on a summer porch, Nancy knew its story in the same way that she writes all her stories—it fell into her mind as though it were always there, yet influenced by the women's march in January 2017. Nancy resides in Harbeson, Delaware, having moved there from Baltimore to be active in the writers' community developed by the Guild.

Mary Ellen South is a retired educator, entrepreneur, public relations and time management specialist who lives in Lewes, Delaware. She has been published in several national periodicals and Virginia newspapers. She and her husband have lived in seven different states and travelled all over the world. Currently, Mary Ellen is working on her book of poetry, *Life in Verse*.

Gayla Sullivan enjoys writing about certain places and how they hold meaning in people's lives. A resident of Salisbury, Maryland, she has taught in southern Delaware for over twenty-five years. Gayla likes to travel, kayak, read, bicycle around Delmarva, and spend time with her family. Having taught first graders for many years, she finds great satisfaction in teaching young children how to read and enjoy books. "Sandrilene Looks Back" is her first published short story.

Marjorie F. Weber, a resident of Lewes, Delaware since 2007, is an active member and serves as webmaster of the Rehoboth Beach Writers Guild. In 2013, she was awarded the Delaware Division of the Arts Emerging Artist Fellowship for creative nonfiction and several of her short stories and essays have recently been accepted for publication. Mrs. Weber began her career as a journalist and later was a technical writer and business analyst before retiring and focusing on creative writing. She also serves on the Lewes Senior Center Board of Directors.

Sherri Wright lives in Rehoboth Beach, Delaware after a career in education for at-risk youth at universities and the Federal government. Running, practicing yoga, working out, and volunteering at a center for homeless all figure into her writing. A member of the Rehoboth Beach Writers Guild, her work has been published in the *Hill Rag; Letters from Camp Rehoboth; Inspired by the Poet; Aspiring to Inspire; Words of Fire and Ice; The White Space; Clementine; Panoply; Creative Nonfiction; Rat's Ass Review,* and *District Lines Volume IV.* Her poem "Private Dancer" received an Honorable Mention in the Louisville Literary Arts Poetry Competition, 2016.

Kit Zak—always a lover of the beach—and her husband moved to Lewes, Delaware after retiring from a nearby university. Kit is involved in writing and progressive groups and loves to travel. For over thirty years she and her family have exchanged homes in the US and Europe. She won second place in several poetry contests and her chapbook, *Once Honeysuckle,* will be available this spring.

EDITORIAL BOARD

Sarah Barnett has had careers as a teacher, librarian and lawyer. Now retired, she lives in Rehoboth Beach where she writes essays and short fiction, serves as vice president of the Rehoboth Beach Writers Guild, teaches writing classes and enjoys leading "free writes" for other writers. Her work has appeared in *Delaware Beach Life, Delmarva Review,* and other publications.

Linda Blumner is a member of the Rehoboth Beach Writers Guild and an ardent reader.

Denise Clemons earned a BA in Biopsychology from Vassar College and an MA in Writing from Johns Hopkins University. She is a member of The Rehoboth Beach Writers Guild; Coastal Writers; the Science Fiction & Fantasy Poetry Association; and the Eastern Shore Writers Association. Denise has published fiction, nonfiction and poetry in journals, chapbooks and anthologies. She writes a weekly food column and her book *A Culinary History of Southern Delaware* was published in 2016.

Maribeth Fischer is the author of two novels, *The Language of Goodbye* (Dutton 2001), and *The Life You Longed For* (Simon & Schuster, 2007) She has published essays in such journals as *The Iowa Review, Creative Nonfiction* and *The Yale Review* and has received two Pushcart Prizes for her essays: "Stillborn," 1994 and "The Fiction Writer," 2014. Maribeth founded the Rehoboth Beach Writers Guild (RBWG) in 2005, where she currently serves as Executive Director. She teaches classes in both novel writing and creative nonfiction for the RBWG.

Cynthia Hall is a freelance marketing and technical writer in Lewes, Delaware with a thirty-year career in corporate communications. Her creative nonfiction work has been published in *Delaware Beach Life* as well as various nonprofit organization publications. Cynthia's foray into fiction writing is well supported by membership in the RBWG, as well as the Eastern Shore Writers Association.

Ethan Joella teaches English and psychology at University of Delaware and runs his own business that specializes in writing workshops and online instruction. His work has appeared in *Best New Writing 2008*; *The International Fiction Review*; *The MacGuffin*; *Rattle*; *Delaware Beach Life*; *and The Delmarva Review*. His book of poetry *Where Dads Go* won second honorable mention and was published by Finishing Line Press.

Bonnie L. Walker, PhD, University of Maryland, is the author of a series of language arts textbooks published by Pearson in their 5th edition, as well as numerous training materials for long-term care staff related to injury prevention, fire safety, and restorative care. Her most recent publication is *A Visit to India*, available in print and ebook from Amazon. Bonnie, a teacher for twelve years, worked at Gallaudet as a curriculum developer, and has received many grants from NIA for research related to aging. She has resided in Rehoboth Beach for seventeen years and is now working on a memoir about her brother.

71916379R00152

Made in the USA
Columbia, SC
10 June 2017